ISLAND INTRIGUE

A Mango Bay Mystery

Other books by Marty Ambrose:

The *Mango Bay Mystery* Series:

Peril in Paradise

ISLAND
INTRIGUE

•

Marty Ambrose

AVALON BOOKS
NEW YORK

Published by Thomas Bouregy & Co., Inc.
160 Madison Avenue, New York, NY 10016

Library of Congress Cataloging-in-Publication Data

Ambrose, Marty.
  Island intrigue / Marty Ambrose.
      p. cm.
  ISBN 978-0-8034-9998-0 (hardcover)
  1.   Women journalists—Fiction.   2. Women detectives—
Fiction.   3. Kidnapping—Fiction. 4. Florida—Fiction.
I. Title.
  PS3601.M368I84 2010
  813'.6—dc22

                                                      2009025923

                    PRINTED IN THE UNITED STATES OF AMERICA
                              ON ACID-FREE PAPER
              BY HADDON CRAFTSMEN, BLOOMSBURG, PENNSYLVANIA

I would like to thank my family, as always, for being my best friends and best critics—especially my husband, Jim, and my mother. They are always ready to offer suggestions and proofreading expertise.

I also have to thank my agent, Roberta Brown, for giving me generous encouragement and professional insight at every step of my writing career. My success is largely due to her.

And I could not wish for a better editor than Faith Black; her revision suggestions truly improve my work at every level. Thank you!

My gratitude and love to the late Mr. Murphy, who taught me about the martial arts and life. I miss you.

Oh, what a tangled web we weave,
When first we practice to deceive. . . .
–Sir Walter Scott, *Marmion*

"The deceiver is one of the best known and
oldest fly patterns in fly-fishing."

Chapter One

"I'd sell my soul for a decent news story," my editor, Anita Sanders, muttered as she kicked the dented wastebasket near my desk. "Just gimme a little arson job. A robbery. Cripes, I'd even settle for a carjacking at this point." She turned to me, tossing last week's edition of the *Coral Island Observer* onto my desk. "I can't take another article about that stupid bike-path controversy. What's our lead for next week?"

I swiveled my computer monitor in her direction. "Tonight's Town Hall meeting. From the agenda, it looks like they're going to cover a lot of scintillating stuff—the possible purchase of a swing set and two new kiddie picnic tables for the island park."

"Ugh." She popped a piece of mint gum into her mouth—the kind that's supposed to help you stop

1

smoking by supplying a tiny amount of nicotine, though not nearly enough for a two-pack-a-day habit. "I can't take one more boring front page. It's killing me."

I was tempted to point out that her high-anxiety reaction to cutting out the cigarette habit might be the cause of some of her dissatisfaction, but I decided to keep my mouth shut. Life was tough enough for Anita as editor of a small-time, weekly newspaper on Coral Island after her stint as a junior reporter for the *Detroit Free Press*. I'd often been moved to pity her present double-intensity stress the last couple of weeks, but then she'd trash one of my stories for the umpteenth time, and I'd feel secret glee at her nicotine withdrawal and journalistic purgatory.

"This paper is a joke, and this office is a dump." She tossed her gum into the wastebasket and unwrapped another piece. I took a quick peek to check that her used gum had actually made it into the can. I'd been stepping on gooey leftovers for the last month and was tired of scraping them off my sandals. Luckily, her aim had proved accurate this time.

I tilted back in my chair, careful not to place my weight over the missing roller on the left rear leg. The office furniture had been purchased from a local flea market eons ago; it had the look of tacky faux oak and creaked with every movement. "Anita, it's after six. Everyone's gone, and I've got to be at my martial arts class in about twenty minutes. Then I have to spend two hours covering a boring Town Hall meeting. Can we save this conversation for later?"

Her wrinkled, thin face sagged into a frown. "Fine, but you'll never win a Pulitzer by keeping bankers' hours." She strode out of the office, slamming the front door behind her.

I shrugged and shut down my computer.

An hour later I was wishing myself back in the office as I lay sprawled facedown on a padded mat, thumping it with my open palm—the universal martial arts signal to let up. "Okay, Sam, you made your point. I left myself open to your attack." I was going to end up double-jointed if he didn't remove his knee from my back and loosen his hold on my arm—pronto. Besides, I could hear the Jordan sisters giggling, and I didn't want to prolong the indignity. Sixteen-year-old twins and incredibly limber, they spent most of their time in Tae Kwon Do class snickering at my awkward attempts to learn self-defense moves.

"Good job," Sam said as he released me.

"Easy for you to say. You've got two working arms." I struggled to my feet as I massaged my shoulder. "Could you give me a heads-up next time before you squash my face into the mat?"

Sam smiled and shook his head. "An opponent won't give you that courtesy—trust me. The first rule in Tae Kwon Do is, always be ready for an attack. It can come from anywhere and anyone. You have to be alert to your surroundings at all times." He straightened his *do bohk*—the white cotton pants and jacket that were de rigeur for class. Their appearance is supposed to symbolize the "way," the absence of ego, but secretly I thought we looked like escapees from an overly zealous chef's school. The belt helped a little, but since mine was white, it hardly made a difference.

"Let's call it a night," Sam said.

All I could do was nod in mute gratitude as our class moved into the final, formal bow.

How did I, Mallie Monroe, late twenty-something motormouth extraordinaire who got all squeamish when I had to kill a bug with a rolled-up fashion magazine, end up face-to-face learning mortal combat in a Tae Kwon Do class?

Since coming to Coral Island on the southwest coast of Florida, I'd done a lot of things that I never would've imagined possible. I'd settled into a job as a reporter for the local island newspaper, I'd created a semipermanent home for myself at the Twin Palms RV Resort; and I'd helped solve the murder of a local writer.

It was that last item on the list that had propelled me into the twice-weekly Tae Kwon Do humiliation. I'd almost been shot and dumped in an archaeological pit—saved only by my own desperation and the quick thinking of island curmudgeon Everett Hall.

Not that I expected to be confronting psycho killers at every turn of a corner, but, in the course of writing my newspaper stories for the last six months, I'd been yelled at, shoved, and on the receiving end of a wide variety of obscene hand gestures, some of which I'd never seen before. Not to mention that I'd had a chocolate chip ice cream cone shoved down the back of my blouse and my butt pinched during a Town Hall meeting. In all fairness, the ice cream incident might've been an accident because my attacker—Old Man Brisbee—had just been diagnosed with macular degeneration and couldn't see too well as he strolled around with the cone. As for the butt pinch, I think Brisbee knew exactly what he was doing.

I'd realized a little self-defense might come in handy—especially if I intended to deflect the crazies I met on the job and keep out of the way of flying chocolate chip ice cream cones.

My great-aunt Lily, grande dame of Coral Island, was the one who'd suggested the Tae Kwon Do. She'd seen a television program about a martial artist somewhere between fifty and a hundred and fifty years old who'd chopped through four concrete blocks with his bare hand and taken on a gang all by his lonesome. He'd probably broken every bone in every finger and acquired a few gray hairs, but she was impressed. I was skeptical but willing to give it a try. Hey, it couldn't hurt.

That's what I'd thought—at first.

It did hurt—a lot. And not just my body. My ego took a bruising in every class, leaving it permanently black and blue.

When I'd signed up at the Island Fitness Center for

Tae Kwon Do, I wasn't the least bit surprised when Sam showed up as the instructor the first night. Of medium height, bald with a gold stud in his left ear, he looked like a cross between a pirate and the Dalai Lama. He had to be almost sixty, but his wide-chested body was trim and fit, each muscle finely tuned. He wore his *do bohk* and black belt with quiet pride yet with total self-command. Known around the island as the "metaphysical handyman," Sam had a Zen-like attitude toward everything from fixing a broken screen to understanding the meaning of life. He also possessed a wicked sense of humor that offset the philosophical bent. Or maybe enhanced it.

"We each have our own potential." Sam turned to me as the class members trailed out. "First you have to know what it is; then you can develop it to its natural end. Some martial artists can walk across nails or bend steel bars. Some can kick ten feet in the air. Some just like to kick the hell out of people. The point is not to do the impossible but to find out what *is* possible. In your case . . ." He trailed off with a grin.

"I'll be lucky to bend a paper clip," I finished for him.

"Not exactly. You'll surprise yourself one day." He winked at me.

I winked back. "See you on Thursday." I grabbed my gym bag and exited the dojo. A chilly blast of wind greeted me, and I wrapped my arms around my middle. It was only mid-November, but an unseasonably early cold snap had swept through southwestern Florida a few days ago. It caused islanders to scurry around trying to find suitable cold-weather gear. Since the temperature didn't dip this low all that often, it was hard to come by suitable clothing. Plaid flannel shirts with corduroys cropped up everywhere, along with tattered warm-up suits and the occasional fringed leather jacket.

Unfortunately, my *do bohk*'s thin white cotton didn't provide much warmth.

I hurried toward my truck, Rusty, which stood parked between Sam's immaculate Volvo and the Jordan sisters' cherry-red Mustang convertible. I always noted what make and model vehicle people drove. To me, cars were more psychologically revealing than Rorschach or word association. Besides, it was fun to play "car shrink." Sam obviously enjoyed sturdy reliability and had no interest in fads or frills. The Jordan sisters' vehicle screamed "two cool chicks."

Rusty was neither particularly attractive nor cool. But he could pull my 4,225-pound antique Airstream trailer and never failed me when the chips were down. Oh, sure, sometimes the window wouldn't open or the door would jam, but my battered truck had heart. Most cars were merely engine and chassis. Mine had personality. It also showed I was living from paycheck to paycheck and couldn't afford a decent paint job.

I drove out of the parking lot at the fitness center and turned onto Cypress Road, the main drag of Coral Island. This little piece of Florida paradise was twenty miles long and about a mile wide. It ran north and south, tucked behind a ring of upscale, tourist-laden barrier islands. Neither upscale nor a magnet for tourists, Coral Island boasted one hotel, a tiny beach, and assorted communities. Originally a homesteaders' haven, Coral Island maintained its rural ambiance. People made a living from the land and sea. They prided themselves on their fierce independence and quirky lifestyle.

I fit right in.

Except I didn't wear the knee-high white fishermen boots known as "island Reeboks." Otherwise, I could be mistaken for a native. Sort of.

Not that most islanders saw me as such. I was a long way from being accepted, even if I had played a small part in clearing the name of a local fisherman who'd been accused of murder last summer. I was still new to the island and, therefore, treated with a certain degree of suspicion.

I cranked up Rusty's heater, and a gust of warmth poured from the vents. My truck might not have air-conditioning, but it possessed a heating unit second to none. In no time a toasty feeling flooded through me.

Reluctantly I headed for the Town Hall meeting.

It was almost eleven o'clock by the time I drove up to the Twin Palms RV Resort at Mango Bay, the northern-most tip of the island.

I parked in front of my shiny silver Airstream trailer, which occupied one of the choice spots only five hundred feet from the tiny strip of sand that passed for a beach. Areca palms decorated the grassy parts, and I'd planted a small bougainvillea, which was in full scarlet bloom. I noticed that the site to my right remained empty.

Then my eyes widened as my glance traveled to the site on my other side. Taking up almost the whole space stood a forty-foot Wanderlodge LX. I'd only read about this particular RV, never actually seen one with its rich, metallic bronze body and fancy black trim. Almost the size of a Greyhound bus, it was sleek and outfitted with the finest accessories—awnings on all the windows, double slide-outs, and a scenic mural of the Rocky Mountains on the back. Wow.

A tap on my window startled me out of my awed fascination. I turned my head and switched off Rusty's engine. It was Wanda Sue—owner, general manager, and one-woman gossip grapevine of the Twin Palms.

I opened my door and slid out. "Kinda late for you to be out and about, isn't it?" I asked, folding my arms to keep from shivering.

"Slap me for being a fool if I don't know it. Brrrr!" she exclaimed, pulling her yellow flannel shirt tightly around her plump body. Two sturdy legs encased in tight black leggings peeped out beneath the shirttails. Farther down, white socks and pink high-heeled sandals completed her ensemble. "It's cold enough to freeze the palmetto bugs right off the trees."

"I'll say." I wasn't sure how cold it needed to get to freeze palmetto bugs, but I guessed we were approaching it. "Who owns the RV behemoth next to me?"

"Can't tell you. It's real hush-hush." She lowered her voice to a whisper. "All I can say is that you'd recognize them if you saw them."

"A famous couple?"

"Maybe."

"Movie stars? Country-western singers?" I couldn't help the eagerness that lit my voice.

"Possibly." Wanda Sue made a locking-key motion in front of her mouth and said nothing else.

Oh, great. What a time for the island's biggest busybody to turn mute.

She patted her new canary-yellow bob in self-satisfaction. I was always amazed at how each evolving hairstyle remained in rigid formation, no matter what the weather. She could stand in a tropical-force wind, and not a hair blew out of place.

"Brad Pitt and Angelina Jolie?"

She shook her head.

"You know, word is going to get out on the island that you've got a famous couple staying here. . . ."

"I promised to protect their privacy, so please don't pass it on."

"All right." I scanned the Wanderlodge again. Lights were on inside, but the shades were drawn. Wouldn't you just know it? I couldn't make out anything or anyone. Then something occurred to me. "If I guess correctly, would you tell me if I'm right?"

She paused. "Okay—deal."

We shook on it.

Wanda Sue lingered, shifting from foot to foot. She cleared her throat. She sniffed. Then she cleared her throat again.

"Wanda Sue, is something wrong?" I asked.

"Maybe—I don't know for sure."

"What's up?"

"It's my daughter, Sally Jo. She's married . . . well, sort of. She and her husband, Tom Crawford, are separated right now." She frowned, a shadow of pain crossing her face. "They'd been getting some counseling from a shrink on the mainland, and things had improved. They were talking about getting back together. But then, out of blue, Tom up and disappears with their son, Kevin."

"Did he kidnap the boy?"

"I don't know. It was Tom's day to pick up Kevin from school and drop him off at Sally Jo's house. He swung by the school about three o'clock, got Kevin, but then never showed up at Sally Jo's trailer."

"When was that?"

"Today. I know it seems kinda alarmist, but you can't be too careful when it comes to kids."

"Did Sally Jo call Detective Billie?" He was the island's chief lawman. A rugged, reserved, by-the-book, kind of cop who also just happened to exude sexy masculinity out of every pore.

Wanda Sue shook her head. "She isn't really sure they're missing."

"Did she try to call Tom?"

"Yep. No answer."

A gust of wind whipped my hair across my face. "Is it possible they took off for a few days and just didn't tell Sally Jo?"

"That's what I told her. They might've gone fishing, and Tom forgot to mention it. I swear, that man wouldn't remember his own birthday if Sally Jo didn't remind him."

"You think they could've gone fishing in this weather? Isn't there an advisory out?"

"Maybe." Wanda Sue's concerned eyes met my glance squarely. I had my answer.

"What can I do?"

"Poke around. See if you can find out if anything has happened to 'em." She touched my arm. "I wouldn't ask, Mallie, except that Sally Jo is practically beside herself with worry, and I don't know who else to turn to. You figured out who murdered that writer guy last summer— digging and digging until you found the truth."

And almost got myself killed, I added to myself.

"I sure would appreciate it, honey." Her voice broke.

"Okay. I'm covering the Autumn Festival at the elementary school tomorrow, so I'll see if anybody knows anything."

"Thanks a million," she gushed. "You're a real friend."

A slow smile spread across my face. "I don't suppose you'd like to rethink letting me in on the identity of my new neighbors."

"No can do."

My smile disappeared. "It was worth a try."

Wanda Sue shook her head as she tottered off. I watched her hair recede into the night like a yellow beacon, and a little voice inside my head told me I was getting myself into something more complicated than an errant husband. Nothing was ever that simple on Coral Island.

My editor, Anita, just might have her wish for a decent news story after all.

Chapter Two

I awoke the next morning to the familiar, slightly icky sensation of a long, slobbery tongue being drawn across my face. "Kong, please." My eyes fluttered open, beholding all 2.8 pounds of my apricot-colored teacup poodle. He was on the small side even for a miniature canine dust mop, so I'd named him—on the recommendation of a doggy psychologist—after the fearsome giant ape in hopes that he'd outgrow his passive-aggressive behavior.

So far my plan hadn't worked.

He still took on strangers as if he were a German shepherd in his aggressive moods but then had to be dragged down to the shoreline for a simple walk along the surf in his passive moments. Whoever heard of a dog who terrorized people but panicked at the thought

14

of dipping one paw into the water? He could've been playing mind games with me, but I wasn't sure. I had my suspicions, though.

Right now Kong was my only companion, so I overlooked his slight personality disorder.

He began to lick my ear.

"Enough already." I threw back the covers and shivered. Rubbing my hands together, I made a beeline for the thermostat. "Jeez. It must've dipped almost to freezing last night." I jerked the lever upward toward seventy. Nothing happened. I toggled it a few times and tapped on the plastic thermostat cover. Heat finally blasted out of the floor grates. Raising my eyes to heaven, I gave a silent prayer of thanks to the heat gods. My Airstream might be refurbished, but it was over twenty years old and didn't like freezing weather any more than I did.

Kong barked.

I groaned, knowing what I had to do. I threw on a pair of tattered sweatpants and an old white cable-knit sweater I'd bought at the island consignment shop. It specialized in "pre-owned" clothing, rather than "used" items. I didn't care what they were called as long as the price was right.

I fastened Kong's leash to his collar and led him outside. A brisk wind roared in from the Gulf of Mexico, the kind that made your teeth chatter and your shoulders hunch up somewhere near your ears. "Get the lead out, Kong. I'm freezing."

He trotted off toward a clump of areca palm trees,

and I cast a quick glance toward the Wanderlodge. The shades up, I could see outlines of objects inside the RV but nothing more. I checked the license plate. It was temporary—the paper kind issued for a new vehicle with *State of Florida* stamped on it. A clue! They'd bought it in state.

"I've got it. Gloria Estefan and her husband—they live in Miami!" I exclaimed to Kong.

He ignored me. A gopher tortoise lumbering toward the beach area had caught his attention, and he kept jumping on its hard-shelled back.

Just then strains of jazz emanated from the Wanderlodge.

No Latin beat. Okay, so it probably wasn't Gloria Estefan and hubby. Then I realized that, just because it was bought in state, that didn't mean the owners lived in Florida. They could've flown in from anywhere, plunked down a quarter of a million dollars at some RV megastore, and driven off into the sunset.

I sighed. *Must be nice.*

Another gust of wind pierced my sweater, and all thoughts of divining my neighbors' identity flew out of my mind. *Yikes.*

I pulled on Kong's leash to distract him from attacking the gopher tortoise. "Let's get down to business, buddy. I've lost all feeling in my fingers."

He wagged his tiny tail, smug in the warmth of his apricot fur.

"It's either here and now, or we make for the *beach*." I flashed him a warning glance.

His head swiveled in my direction. I nodded and repeated the dreaded *b* word again. He did his thing, and we retreated back to the Airstream before I could say, "Surf's up."

I showered and made my way out to my truck in less than half an hour. I didn't spend a lot of time on makeup and fancy clothing. To be honest, I didn't have much of either. Occasional lipstick and powder comprised my normal "made-up" face. As for clothes, I wore jeans and a T-shirt in the summer, jeans and a sweater in the winter. Simple and cheap.

But I did devote at least fifteen minutes a day to my hair. It was my one vanity. I fluffed the scarlet curls with loving care until they shone like a new tomato. Unfortunately, I had the sun-sensitive, freckled skin that often went with that color hair, but I figured my rich, luxurious tresses were nature's way of compensating me.

Not that there was a man in sight to admire them, if you didn't count Old Man Brisbee with his bushy eyebrows and protruding stomach. And the only reason he'd probably started flirting with me was because he felt guilty about the ice cream incident. Or maybe he liked the feel of my butt.

As I drove Rusty along Cypress Drive toward the *Observer* office, a tiny voice reverberated in my head: *Don't forget Detective Billie.*

As if I could. But he certainly seemed to have forgotten about me.

Once the murder case had been solved a few months ago, he hadn't so much as called me to see if I had recovered. Oh, sure, I'd seen him at the Town Hall meetings, but he always came in late and left early, without so much as a "hi-ho" to me. I'd been tempted to drop by the police station on some trumped-up pretext, like a jaywalking alligator, but it seemed lame.

To tell the truth, I didn't know how I felt about him. With his lean-hipped, powerful body and black-as-night eyes, he made my heart beat like a heavy metal drum every time I saw him. But he also ticked me off with his arrogant, rigid, my-way-or-the-highway kind of attitude. *What's an independent kind of girl like me to do?*

I braked for the slow zone near the elementary school. Seeing the flashing yellow of the signal light and watching the school guard help the kids cross the road made me think of Wanda Sue's missing grandson again.

I made a mental note to talk to Kevin's teacher when I came back to do the story on the Autumn Festival. But first I had to check in with Anita.

As I breezed into the *Observer* office, I was assailed by the smell of fresh paint. Much to my amazement, a tall, heavyset young guy was applying a coat of seafoam-colored paint to the back wall. As I closed the door, he grinned and waved his brush in my direction.

"What's going on?" I questioned Sandy, our secretary-cum-receptionist-cum advertising manager-cum-everything.

"Can you believe it? Mr. Benton—the cheapo guy who owns the paper—called this morning and said we could finally get the place painted." She waved one pudgy hand in the direction of the painter. A price tag fell out of the sleeve of her soft yellow sweater. She tucked it back in as though it were simply a loose thread. In the process of losing weight on her latest diet, she was working her way down clothing sizes. Never sure how long she'd be "plateaued" at a certain size, she liked to hedge her bets and be able to return items at a moment's notice. Personally, it struck me as borderline unethical, but she'd lost over twenty pounds in the last year, and I didn't want to discourage her.

"Of course, Anita didn't waste any time. She got a painter over here pronto and let me pick out the color. I decided on this one 'cause one of my New-Age magazines said the sea is restful, serene. Just the kind of background to counteract the high energy of a newspaper."

"Good idea." *High energy*? This was a three-woman operation, for goodness' sake (and Anita barely counted as female). But I had to admit that anything would be an improvement to our shabby workplace. Dulled yellow linoleum graced our floor, two wooden desks, back-to-back, served as our workstations, and a single fluorescent light hummed above our heads.

Being a weekly paper with limited circulation, the

Observer didn't pull in big advertising dollars, needless to say. Whiteside's General Store at Mango Bay was our largest client, and considering the fact that their establishment wasn't much bigger than a convenience store, they didn't spend big bucks promoting their two-for-one toothpaste specials.

In even worse condition than the main area was Anita's space, a glass-enclosed cubicle. As editor of the paper, she possessed the only office—a ten-by-ten cubbyhole that barely provided space for a desk and a couple of chairs. Most of the time she sat in there obsessively checking wire services and hoping for hot-breaking island news that rarely happened.

"What does Anita think of the color?" I asked.

Sandy shrugged. "She hates it, but she hates everything, so I guess that means it's okay."

Made sense to me.

"Hey, kiddo." Speak of the devil. Anita appeared in the doorway of her office. "Did you cover the Town Hall meeting last night?" The only person I knew who could do this, she blew her nicotine gum into a bubble, then burst it with a loud smack. *Charming.*

I nodded. "Big doings, let me tell you. It took them two hours to agree to buy the swing set and picnic tables. Then Old Man Brisbee pinched my cheek again—and I don't mean my face."

"Don't tell me. . . . He's still using that cataract excuse?"

"Macular degeneration."

She grunted in disgust. "Brisbee has been using that one for years. The old fool just likes pinching women's rear ends. He tried it on me years ago, and I grabbed his arse right back."

"Next time I see him, I'll make sure my butt is nowhere in his vicinity."

"Good idea." She eyed the painter for a few seconds, and her mouth tightened, causing the multitude of vertical smoker's lines to deepen. I couldn't tell whether she was smiling or grimacing. "What do you think of our decorating job? Benton decided to pump some money into fixing up our office, so I jumped on it before he changed his mind. Of course the only thing that really counts is putting out a good paper."

"True, but the place does look kinda grungy. And bluish green is a nice color," I pointed out.

"I guess—if you're into that kind of crap. The smell alone is enough to make me gag."

I blinked in amazement. Was it possible that her sense of smell was still intact after daily sessions of breathing in nothing but heavy-duty, lung-scarring tobacco smoke?

"Write that Town Hall story—and the Autumn Festival piece you're covering today. I'll need to check 'em both over before Friday's deadline." She cleared her throat. "This damn gum isn't doing anything—I'd walk across a beach of broken seashells for a cigarette right now."

A tiny pang of sympathy nagged at me. "Maybe you could try the nicotine patch."

She muttered an expletive and retreated into her office, slamming shut the door.

I raised my eyes to the ceiling and groaned to Sandy, "I'm sorry about her cigarette cravings, but I can't believe she still wants to edit *every* line of my stories." I thumped my large canvas bag onto the desk. Two pens and a can of Diet Coke rolled out. I shoved them back into the black hole that passed for my purse. "I've been working here almost six months, and I think I can write a simple story without her second-guessing everything I've done."

"Anita is a Capricorn, ruled by Saturn." A smile tipped the corners of Sandy's bow-shaped mouth. "She likes control and order. . . . You have to let her do her thing, or she'll feel like she's losing her sense of authority."

"Do you know her rising sign?" the painter piped up.

We both turned in his direction.

"Huh?" I couldn't imagine anything "rising" out of Anita except curses and mutterings.

"My mom is Madame Geri—short for Geraldine." He placed a hand across his heart and, in a quaint, old-fashioned gesture, gave a slight bow.

"Our newspaper astrologer?" I asked.

"Yep. And I gotta tell you, she knows her stuff. Really awesome. She taught me a lot about the planets and how they influence people."

Sandy's features kindled in sudden interest. "I *love* Madame Geri's column. I mean, she isn't just your average, run-of-the-mill astrologer. She . . . she's *clairvoyant.*"

I listened to the two of them praising Madame Geri for a few minutes, wondering if they were talking about the same person whose column rarely said anything more specific than *Avoid arguments today and you'll feel much happier.* Who couldn't predict that?

"If I could get the date and time of Anita's birth, do you think Madame Geri could do her chart?" Sandy asked, her voice rising in excitement.

"Sure," he said.

"But, Sandy—" I began.

"No 'but's about it. Listen, Mallie, if we can find out what makes Anita tick, it could make things work a lot smoother around here," Sandy pointed out.

"I don't think—"

"It could even help you find a way to get your articles written without her breathing down your neck."

She had me there. "I . . . I guess there's nothing wrong with just checking out her birth date."

"I'll get right on it—after my diet bar." Sandy pulled out a six-inch bar with the words LOW CALORIE blazoned across the silver foil.

"Are you dieting?" the painter asked.

Sandy chomped a large bite out of her bar and nodded.

"Me too." He gestured toward his potbelly. A youngish guy probably in his midtwenties, he had the beefy good looks of a guy who ate his frosted cereal flakes every morning rather than checking to see if his planets were aligned.

As they conversed about the merits of their present

diet for a few minutes, I rooted around in my desk drawer for my Official Reporter's Notepad. Once I found it, I tossed it into my canvas bag along with the new addition to my journalist's arsenal: an iPod. I thought it gave me a certain panache to whip it out when I was conducting interviews. As long as I remembered to hit Record and then Save.

"I'm driving over to the elementary school now." I threw a couple of extra pens into my bag, since I still primarily took hard-copy notes. "Let me know if anyone calls."

"Will do," Sandy said absently. Elbows propped on the desk, she was still absorbed in her conversation with the cute painter.

I grabbed my bag, zipped my cheap blue Windbreaker right up to my chin, and ran out to my truck. As I pulled out of the parking lot, I glanced over at the small police station that stood alone across the road. A neatly landscaped, one-story, wood-frame building, it looked like Detective Billie—sleek and remote. I imagined his sitting at his desk, methodically sifting through paperwork. That little vertical line between his eyes would appear as he frowned in concentration. He might even shove his dark, straight hair back from his forehead with an impatient hand—

A horn honked.

"Get a move on, missy. We don't have all day!" a gray-haired man with a beard shouted from the car behind me.

"Oh, jeez, it's Everett Hall," I said aloud. The island curmudgeon. He saved my life a few months ago but somehow negated that by always making a habit of being cranky to the point of downright obnoxious in my presence. *Coot.* I flicked my turn signal and pulled out onto Cypress Road. He turned the other way before I could make a rude hand gesture.

Within a few minutes I stood in the main office of the Coral Island Elementary School. A bustling place, it was the preferred school for most of the island kids. A few people from the ritzy Sea Belle Isle Point area drove their children into private schools in town, but most Coral Islanders preferred that their kids attend the island school. Painted a hot shade of mango, the one-story, stuccoed building hummed with energy and warmth.

"Hi, Trisha," I said to the receptionist. She flashed a wide smile in my direction. With her shoulder-length, nut brown hair and open features, she looked little older than most of the kids.

"Hi yourself." She handed me a steaming cup of coffee. "Cold enough for you?"

"I'll say." I sipped it gratefully. The heat spread through my body. I sighed in contentment.

"Sorry all the donuts are gone."

"Shoot." She'd learned all my weaknesses from the many times I'd come here to do stories.

"I think I've got a couple of oatmeal cookies in my purse."

"Forget it. 'A rose by any other name . . . ' "

"Huh?"

"Shakespeare said it in his play, *Romeo and Juliet* . . . uh . . . never mind." Sometimes my degree in comparative literature would rear its ugly head, and I'd feel compelled to make a literary allusion. Usually no one responded, except with diffidence. Today, you were lucky if people knew that Dickens wasn't some kind of hip-hop band on MySpace. "I'm here to cover the Autumn Festival."

"Great. The kids are in the gym wearing overalls and doing a jump rope marathon."

"Oh, joy."

Tricia had me sign in and handed me a hall pass. "Remember, don't use the kids' restroom. Adults are supposed to use the one designated for teachers."

I rolled my eyes. Last time I visited, I made the mistake of using the little girls' restroom. A couple of kids ratted on me, and the repercussions of that faux pas reverberated all the way back to Anita, who gave me a stern lecture about conducting myself with proper journalistic decorum at all times and in all places. Heck, I was only trying to use the toilet.

"Do you know Wanda Sue's grandson, Kevin?" I asked.

"Yeah, Kevin Crawford. Nice kid. Has a buzz cut and braces."

"Sounds adorable." I shifted my heavy canvas bag from one shoulder to the other. "What's the story with his parents?"

"Not much. Father is barely eking out a living as a fisherman, but that's pretty much every other guy on this island. He and Sally Jo, Kevin's mother, were having domestic problems, and he moved out."

"I heard from Wanda Sue that they were getting back together."

"Maybe. I don't know." She put her elbows on the desk and propped up her chin with her hands. "Why are you asking?"

"Wanda Sue told me last night that Kevin's dad was supposed to pick him up from school and take him over to Sally Jo's house, but he never showed up."

"Oh, yeah, I remember now. Sally Jo called around four o'clock and asked if Kevin's dad had picked him up. I checked with Kevin's teacher, and she said yes."

"What's her name?" I pulled out my Official Reporter's Notepad.

"Beverly Jennings."

I scribbled down her name. "Any other helpful info on the boy?"

"Nope. Except that it's pretty common for an island fisherman to take his kid out of school for a couple of days and go on a boating trip."

"You think that's what happened? In this weather?"

"Dunno."

"Okay, thanks. See ya." I flipped the notepad shut and exited the office. Walking in the direction of the gym, I wondered briefly if Wanda Sue had sent me on a wild goose chase. I told myself I had to cover the festival for the paper anyway, but I secretly still wanted to prove myself to Anita as a real reporter.

It wouldn't be the first time. Some people had a nose for news. A sixth sense for headlines. Whereas I had an instinct for the inane. I thought every half-baked story that came in my direction might be "the big one"—the article that would finally get Anita off my back. *Fat chance.* After the murder case last summer, the best headline I'd been able to write was about the island streaker, a guy who liked to run around naked while he did his laundry. Nothing too earthshaking there, just a man who liked to wash his clothes au naturel.

I shoved my Official Reporter's Notepad back into my canvas bag. In this case, I hoped it *would* be one of those nothing stories, and Kevin would show up at Sally Jo's later today, safe and sound.

I headed for the gym.

Chapter Three

The cacophony of children's voices drew me toward the the gym. As I entered the large room with its high ceiling and shiny wood floors, I stopped in my tracks and blinked twice, not sure if I was ready to take the plunge.

Probably about a hundred overall-clad boys and girls bobbed up and down as they spun neon-colored jump ropes over their heads. Another twenty or so kids appeared to be keeping tallies of each other's jumps, and a few older girls lounged off to one side with water bottles and lemonade pitchers. All of the laughing, talking, and jumping generated enough heat to warm every RV park south of Orlando. And then some.

I had to admit it was a pretty ingenious way to help kids work off their surplus energy.

29

Scanning the room for any sign of an adult, I spied a tall, twentyish blond woman standing near the water and lemonade stand. Even from a distance I noticed her shining fall of light hair. It looked like spun gold, beautifully cut and colored—obviously the work of an expert stylist. My interest was sparked—not because I wanted to dye my red curls but because I desperately needed my mane trimmed and didn't completely trust Trixie, the island's lone beauty parlor operator and part-time electrician. I never knew if I'd come out with a good cut or the urge to rewire a ceiling fan. Or maybe both.

I weaved my way through the jumpers, careful not to be hit by a rogue rope.

"Whew, I didn't think I'd make it through there alive!" I exclaimed as I emerged on the other side of the gym.

"I know what you mean. . . . It's a jungle." The blond smiled. She wore a red wool jumper with a white blouse, opaque tights, and flat black Mary Janes. Had to be the teacher. My glance narrowed as an emblem on the jumper caught my eye. *Uh-oh.* A Mickey Mouse was embroidered on the left side. I shuddered. My short, undistinguished tenure at Disney World had left me with a permanent aversion to the tittering mouse and anyone singing "It's a Small World." Nevertheless, I had to admit that I still sported a watch with a tiny Mickey in the center whose white-gloved hands kept time. I was nothing if not inconsistent.

"I'm Mallie Monroe from the *Observer,*" I said.

"What?" She cupped an ear.

I motioned my head toward an unoccupied corner of the gym. She followed me there. I introduced myself again, explained why I was there, and we shook hands.

"Tell me about the Autumn Festival." I reached for my notepad again, realizing that I'd get bupkes on the iPod with this din in the background.

"This is just one of our planned events. We call it the Island Jumpers—isn't that just adorable?" Her face lit up with excitement. "Kids from kindergarten to fifth grade bring their jump ropes, and they work in teams to raise money for the school. Merchants from the island sponsor them. Last year we made almost three thousand dollars so we could buy some new computers for the library. There's nothing like teamwork. That's what the kids learn. That and love make the world go 'round."

I grimaced inwardly at that last line and scribbled down what she was saying as fast as I could, editing out the cheesy ending.

"It's also a great way to give the kids time off from the regular school day. Balancing work and fun is essential for young students today. That way they don't get their dear little selves burned out."

I looked up. "Burned out? In fourth grade?"

"I'm afraid so. With the new state competency exams, a lot of pressure is put on the kids."

"That hardly seems fair." I guess education had a bottom line just like practically everything else in today's world. Even Disney World had to sell a certain number of tickets to keep the attractions open.

"We have other upcoming events that are supposed to be just pure fun—a fishing tournament and a car wash."

"I'll be sure to cover those." *Oh, great, more hard-hitting news stories.* "What's your name, by the way?"

"Beverly Jennings."

My interest perked up. "What a coincidence. I was going to look you up about another matter."

"Oh?"

"A friend of mine . . . she's actually my landlady, who owns the Twin Palms RV Resort where I stay—"

"Wanda Sue."

I nodded. "She asked me to see if I could find out what happened to her grandson—"

"Kevin." Her eyes clouded in puzzlement. "He's one of my students, but, as far as I know, he was just fine when his father picked him up from school yesterday."

"That's the problem. Kevin's father picked him up and was supposed to drop him at his mother's house—"

"Sally Jo."

"Right." Was she, like, the island name expert, or what? *Jeez.* I took a deep breath and continued. "Anyway, Sally Jo is upset because she hasn't heard anything from Kevin or his father." I pronounced the names with breakneck speed.

"You know they're separated," she supplied in a confidential manner, leaning forward almost to my ear as she continued. "And I've heard they're heading for a *d-i-v-o-r-c-e.*"

Thank you, Tammy Wynette. "Really? My source indicated that they might be getting back together." But that was Wanda Sue, who wasn't the most reliable of informants—especially about her own daughter.

"Maybe so." Beverly pulled back and pursed her mouth. "The important thing is Kevin's well-being. Over the last couple of months I've tried to make sure the dear boy has had a supportive environment here at school while his parents were sorting through their problems."

"I'm sure they appreciated that."

"Kevin did." She nodded in a knowing way.

Okay. "Back to my original question: You don't think anything's amiss with Kevin and his dad?"

She paused. "No. Mainly because his dad has taken him out of school before to go fishing for a few days. Fishermen on the island do that a lot. Obviously we discourage it at the school because it interrupts the kids' academic studies. But the guys do it anyway."

"So you think that's where they are?"

She nodded. "Unfortunately, it happens all the time."

"Did his father actually *say* he was going to take Kevin fishing?" I pressed her.

"Not in so many words . . ."

"But you got the idea that they might be boating for a few days?"

"I saw the fishing poles in the back of his truck."

"Okay, thanks for your input. I'm sure you're right. Wanda Sue is probably being an overprotective granny." I shoved my pen behind my ear. I knew it was a nasty habit, but if I dropped it back into my canvas bag, chances were, I'd never find it again—or the others I'd tossed in. "I'm going to take a few pictures of the kids jumping rope for the newspaper—my editor got it cleared by the principal this morning."

"Sure."

"Oh, by the way, do you mind if I ask where you get your hair done? I've been looking for a good stylist since I came to Coral Island."

"My dad does it." She tucked her hair behind her ears and smiled. "He's a hairdresser in Maimi."

Wouldn't ya know? No way could I afford to drive to Miami to get my hair trimmed. "Thanks anyway." I'd have to bite the bullet and stick it out with Trixie. At the very least I might learn how to monitor my Airstream's electrical system.

I took a deep breath and plunged into the hoard of jump rope-wielding kids. I spent a few minutes snapping pictures, making sure I caught a variety of ages and boys as well as girls. When I was ready to leave, I noticed a group of older boys, probably around eleven or twelve, hovering near the entrance to the gym. As I passed them, one in particular gave me a hard stare. Tall for his age, with a crew cut and sullen features, he stood out because he was probably the only person in the gym who appeared not to be having a good time.

"Hi," I said. He ignored me. "Hi," I repeated in a louder tone.

He mumbled something that could've been "Hullo" or "Hell, no."

"Where are your jump ropes?" I asked the boys.

"Those are for girls and wusses," they responded in unison.

"Yeah, I guess so. I'd probably feel the same way if I were you."

A couple of the boys looked at me with a glimmer of interest. Except the sullen one. His eyes remained dark and insolent.

"This whole thing is dumb," he muttered.

"But it raises money for your school," I said. "That's good, isn't it?"

"My dad says school is for them who can't do nothing else," the boy continued. "I want to be a fisherman like him. I don't need no school learning to toss a bait net."

The other boys began to murmur among themselves and shifted away from us.

"I didn't like school much when I was your age, but down the road I realized that I was wrong. My parents always wanted me to be at the top of the class—which I never was, and that made me really resent the kids who were. I thought school was supposed to be fun. A place where I could talk to other kids and hang out on the playground. But it turned out to be a lot of work, and I didn't like that. So, I can see how you might not want to sit in a classroom all day—especially when you could be outside on a boat, fishing and having a good time." I paused, surprised at my diatribe. For some reason my motormouth had clicked into gear. *Must be all the jump rope energy.* "You might be surprised at what education can do for you."

Some of the sullen expression cleared out of his face. "You sure talk a lot."

"Yeah, I know. It's genetic."

"Huh?"

"Never mind." I held out my hand. "I'm Mallie. What's your name?"

"Robby."

"Nice to meet you, Robby." We shook hands. "I work for the island newspaper, and I'm doing a story about the Autumn Festival. You want me to quote you?"

"You mean put what I say in the paper?"

"Yep." I whipped out my Official Reporter's Notepad again and retrieved my pen.

"Cool."

"What do you think of the festival so far this year?" I gave him an encouraging nod.

"It's . . . okay."

"Good answer." I jotted it down. "Anything else?"

He looked down. A few seconds passed. "Nope, I guess not."

"All right." I tossed the notepad back into my canvas bag. "See ya around, Robby." I smiled at him and started to leave.

"Were you asking Miz Jennings about Kevin?" he asked.

I stopped dead in my tracks. "Yes, as a matter of fact, I was. How did you know?"

"I dunno." He shrugged. "Just guessed that he might be in trouble."

"Did Kevin say anything to you?"

"Nah, he's only a fourth-grader—just a little guy. I'm in the fifth grade." He thumped his chest in pride. "But I heard that he was afraid his dad would find out about some stuff that he was doing around the island."

" 'Stuff'? Like what?"

"Stealing . . . breaking windows. Things like that."

"Oh, *that* kind of stuff." Interesting that Wanda Sue had neglected to pass on this piece of information. "He isn't in trouble as far as I know—yet."

Robby shrugged.

"Did he say *why* he was stealing or breaking windows?"

"I . . . uh . . ."

"Robby, stop blabbering and wasting the lady's time." A burly man yanked on the boy's shoulder. He sported an identical crew cut and sullen expression, so I guessed he was Robby's father.

"He wasn't wasting my time. I asked him—" I began.

"I heard what you asked him," he interrupted. "My boy don't have nothing to do with Kevin Crawford."

"But—" I held up a hand.

"Let's go, son." He maneuvered Robby away from me and toward the lemonade stand. The other boys followed.

"Call me at the newspaper if you can think of anything else," I said to their retreating backs.

Talk about rude—and a creepo excuse for a father. I tossed my pen and notepad into my canvas bag and headed out.

Exiting the gym, I thought about what Robby had said. Was Kevin a budding juvenile delinquent? If so, did that have any connection with his possible disappearance? It didn't seem likely, but I'd learned that things weren't always what they seemed on Coral Island. They were generally worse. And why had Robby's father come on like a heavy in a gangster movie just because I was talking to his son? Did he have something to hide?

I dropped my pass off at the main office and headed out to the parking lot. As a blast of cold wind buffeted me, I folded my arms across my chest and hustled into my truck. I cranked up the engine and sat there a few moments, reveling in the heat pouring out of Rusty's vents. Then I checked my watch. Eleven-thirty. I needed to get back to the *Observer,* finish the Town Hall story, and start working on my Autumn Festival article.

But first I needed to follow up on my investigation into Kevin's possible disappearance.

A few minutes later I walked into the island police station. The small wood-framed building contained a reception area, an office, and two cells. Generally the

most heinous criminal ever locked up was Ned—the island jaywalker who'd stagger out of the Seafood Shanty
around midnight after a few too many beers, singing
rap songs at the top of his lungs. He didn't have a bad
voice, but who wanted to hear rap so late at night?

"Mallie, long time no see," Rhonda, the attractive
brunet receptionist, hailed me. One of those supereffi-
cient, never-a-hair-out-of-place, incredibly organized
women, she should've irritated the heck out of me. But
Rhonda was also a genuinely nice person. Just my luck—
I couldn't even dislike her.

"Cold enough for you?" I strolled over to their
industrial-sized coffeemaker.

"Freezing. I've been in Florida over ten years, and
this is the coldest snap we've ever had this early in the
season. I hate it."

"Me too." I took a long, deep swig of the coffee. *Ah,
strong and black. Just the way I like it.* "Is Detective
Billie in?"

"He is," the man himself answered from the doorway
of his office in all his magnificent masculinity. Okay,
maybe I was exaggerating a little. True, his straight black
hair flowed back from his forehead like dark silk, and his
eyes glowed deeper than a starless night. But his ruggedly
handsome face was set in an expression of stubborn rigid-
ity. So he just missed "magnificent" by a millimeter or
two. But who's counting?

"I . . . I need to ask you a few questions." *Keep cool.*
I mentally fanned myself.

"If it's about last month's Town Hall meeting—"

"No, it's not," I cut in swiftly. When I'd seen him at the October Town Hall meeting—the same one where the infamous chocolate chip ice cream episode had occurred—I proposed that he write a police-beat column for the *Observer* covering crimes that had occurred on the island during the week. Needless to say, he shot me down as if I were a cardboard figure at target practice. "I'm working on a story. Uh . . . not exactly a story. More like a possible story. At least, it could *become* a story if it works out to be true. Although I'm not sure if it is true. I'll only know that if I can find out what happened." I stopped there. My motormouth was slipping a few gears, and I didn't know how to stop it. *Why does he make me so tongue-tied?*

"Come again?" He tilted his head to one side, regarding me as if I were speaking a foreign language.

"Could we go into your office? This *might* be official police business."

He paused. "All right. But I've got a lunch appointment at one. Do you think you could make yourself clear by that time?"

I raised my chin in defiance. "I'm always clear. It's this case that's confusing."

He stood to one side, and I breezed past him with my coffee cup, inhaling the woodsy scent that always seemed to cling to him. It was probably one of those modern colognes with a pseudo-manly name like Brawl or Robust that was supposed to conjure up images of athletic, virile men pumping iron and breathing hard. But they always made me think of superabsorbent paper towels.

Still, Nick Billie sure smelled nice. . . .

After I took a seat, he slid into the chair behind his desk and began in a long-suffering tone, "I know I'm going to regret asking, but what's this all about?"

"Here's the scoop," I answered in a sweet voice. "Wanda Sue asked me if I could help her find her grandson, Kevin. Apparently his dad picked him up from school yesterday, and they never showed up at Sally Jo's house. He was supposed to drop Kevin there. Sally Jo called her husband's house, but there was no answer. She's pretty upset."

"Sally Jo or Wanda Sue?"

"Both, I think."

His mouth twisted wryly.

"You think something could've happened to them?"

"Like what? Like they've gone fishing and not told Sally Jo? I can't tell you the number of times that's happened over the last year. And every time Tom takes off with Kevin like that, Sally Jo calls here and says she's going to file a complaint against him. Then when Tom and Kevin come back in a few days, she forgets all about it—until the next time. My advice is, stay out of it. Don't get between Sally Jo and her husband. They like to play these little games." He leaned back in his chair.

"But this time could be real. Isn't it possible that Tom kidnapped Kevin? That happens with separated dads all the time." I tried not to sound like an alarmist, but I felt a little peeved that he had dismissed my suspicions as if they were no more than the foolish ravings of a woman desperate for any pretext to make contact with him. Then again, was he that far wrong?

"Theoretically anything is possible, but it's not likely—I can tell you that."

"Isn't it better to be safe than sorry?"

"It's better to have reasonable certainty than to go off half-cocked."

"But a young boy's life could be at stake."

He leaned forward. "If I had any real reason to be concerned, I'd turn this island upside down to find Kevin. But I also know that overreacting to every little complaint that comes in does nothing but panic people. And that's the last thing that I want to—"

"But how can you know for sure?"

"I don't." His face turned hard. "I have to use my judgment."

"But everyone makes mistakes—even you."

His brows leveled into a thunderous line. "What has Anita told you?"

"Nothing." It was sort of true. All I knew was that Detective Billie was part Miccosukee and had left the reservation in southern Florida under a cloud.

"Did she say that I made a mistake years ago? Was that it?"

"She might've said something last summer about your leaving a previous job over an . . . unsettling case,

but nothing else." My mouth suddenly felt dry. I cleared
my throat. "She thinks very highly of you. So do I, for
that matter."

His hands clenched and unclenched on top of the
desk. "Sorry. I didn't mean to come on so strong. It all
happened a long time ago, but it's still there in the back
of my mind. My only excuse is that I was young, brash,
and way too full of myself—if that can be called an excuse." A shadow passed across his face, and he lowered
his head. "You move on, but you never really get over
something like that."

Like what? I wanted to scream. But we didn't have
the kind of relationship where he'd reveal his deep,
dark secrets to me.

"Enough of that." He looked up again. "Just to play it
safe, I'll check with Sally Jo after lunch."

"You mean we're in agreement?" I asked in disbelief.

"I guess so."

"Will wonders never cease?"

A ghost of a smile passed across his face. "You know,
when I first met you, I thought you might be a murderer.
Then I thought you were a pain in the—"

"I get the picture." *And* the part of the anatomy he
was going to reference.

"Now, I can't tell if you just like causing trouble or if
it naturally follows you."

"My middle name is Ann, not Trouble." My throat
opened up again, and I could swallow once more.

"I know. You forget that I have a background file on

you. Name, birth date, social security number—I've got a complete picture of Mallie Ann Monroe."

"Surely not everything." I was dying to have a peek into that file. Not that I'd done anything all that bad, but, like everyone else, I had had a few youthful indiscretions. Most of them had had to do with rebelling against my parents and their Midwest values. TP-ing a house at Halloween. Stealing apples from mean old Mrs. Mattelbaum's orchard. Nothing all that earthshaking.

"The only piece of information I'm missing is where you get your hair dyed." His eyes rested on my fire engine red hair.

"It's natural. You can ask my great-aunt Lily. She still calls me Carrot." He might not believe me, but I knew he wouldn't question the word of Great-aunt Lily.

"Carrot?" He laughed. "That's too tame by a long shot. More like Chili Pepper—that fits you."

"As vegetables go, I guess that's a step up. If I didn't know better, Detective Billie, I'd think you were starting to like me."

"But you do know better."

We stared at each other across the desk. Something passed between us. A sensual vibe. A connection. A tentative bond. I don't know what it was. But it left me shaky.

I murmured something and got out of there as fast as my wobbly legs could take me.

Chapter Four

I swung by the Circle K deli and picked up my usual working lunch: a ham and Swiss hoagie, two bags of chips, and a mammoth-sized chocolate chip cookie. I figured I hit most of the food groups with that combo, and what I missed could be made up with two steaming cups of black coffee.

I wolfed down most of the meal in my truck as I drove back to the *Observer* office. With an ease born of long practice, I could drink my coffee, shift with my sandwich hand, and never lose even a shred of lettuce. I often used Rusty as the setting for a moveable feast during the workweek—not because I didn't like to sit down to a meal, but because I didn't want to put undue stress on Sandy as she struggled with her diet, while I struggled with the choice of fries or chips with my triple-decker cheeseburger. Sure, it would catch up with me at some point, but right now I enjoyed guilt-free, fast-food nirvana.

I was savoring the last bite of my hoagie as I strolled into the office. "Sandy, I deserve combat pay for dodging jump ropes—" I broke off in midsentence as I noticed a newcomer seated near Sandy's desk. I blinked a couple of times, making sure that my eyes were focused correctly. Sure enough, a middle-aged woman with grayish dreadlocks, wearing a sundress and pearls, inclined her head toward me. A Rastafarian homemaker. But it wasn't her unusual appearance that got my attention. It was the jewel-toned bird perched on her right shoulder.

"I . . . I thought Anita had a rule about pets in the office," I stammered, scanning the green feathers and pale yellow head.

"Marley's not a pet—he's my familiar." The woman stroked the bird, who fastened two beady eyes on me. "Otherwise he's known as a turquoise-fronted parrot."

I kept my distance. I don't like birds—never have, never will. I was almost attacked by a rogue duck once at summer camp in middle school, and it traumatized me for life.

"Not to worry. Anita is out of the office for the rest of the afternoon. She had to drive into town to meet with Mr. Benton," Sandy chimed in. "This is Madame Geri. After our talk this morning, Jimmy called her, and she came right over."

"Who's Jimmy?"

The painter waved his brush from across the room.

"Right. Gotcha. Madame Geri's son," I said. That made sense, I guess. Not wanting to get too close to the beady-eyed bird, I waved a hand in a friendly hello.

"Sandy said you needed an astrological chart for your boss," the so-called psychic said, arranging the folds of her sundress.

"Yeah . . . uh . . . maybe so . . ." I eased around Madame Geri to reach my desk. "If you have the time, that is." *Please let her schedule be filled.*

"I always have time to study the planets. They're the windows to understanding ourselves and our universe." She gestured in an expansive arc with her hands. "It's not always easy to determine the forces working on us in this life. Sometimes they're complex, sometimes simple. But no matter what, our sun sign is the dominant force in our lives, with our moon and rising signs as lesser influences. Those are the keys to life."

"I howled at the moon once. Does that count?" I offered.

Madame Geri studied me as if I were some type of alien. "You're an Aquarian. You like to be different. Always restless, always on the move. Looking for the next adventure. But recently you've found yourself putting down roots, wanting a home. Your big fear is that life will become one big, dull routine, so you work here for variety."

"Wow. Have you been talking to my mother?" Anyone could've guessed that about me. Especially someone plugged into the island grapevine. It was common knowledge that I lived in an Airstream trailer and had worked my way south with a string of temporary jobs.

Madame Geri gave a contemptuous laugh, causing her dreadlocks to shake. "I don't need to."

I tried to think of another jokè, but I couldn't come up with anything witty. Besides, Madame Geri was now looking at me with the exact same expression as her bird, and it was making me uncomfortable. I turned to Sandy. "Did you dig up Anita's birth date?"

"Sure did." Sandy grinned as she held up an employment application form. "I found this little nugget of history in the files." She scanned it for a few seconds. "Says Anita was born on January 14, 1945."

Madame Geri closed her eyes. "Hmmm. A Capricorn, with maybe a Virgo moon sign. Interesting combination. She likes control, order, runs a tight ship. She can weather a lot of storms, has a dry sense of humor, but her big fear is emotional hurt. She'll do anything to avoid that. And the Virgo moon creates a tension between her needs and desires. She may even have a secret longing for . . ."

"Another job?" Sandy inquired.

"A man in her life?" Jimmy the Painter had abandoned his job and stood behind his mother.

"Nontoxic cigarettes?" I couldn't resist adding.

Madame Geri kept her eyes shut, then opened them and took in a deep breath. "I can't tell. I need to do her chart. Then I'll know for sure."

Damn. I was curious in spite of myself. The image of prune-faced Anita bubbling up inside with a cauldron of hidden desires had piqued my curiosity.

"How long will it take?" I gestured toward the sloppy mess in Anita's office. "You see what we're up against here. She's given up cigarettes, stopped cleaning her office, and is barking out orders like a drill sergeant."

"I need a few days." Madame Geri shrugged. "These things can't be rushed." She rose to her feet, her sundress falling around her rather trim figure in flattering folds. Aside from the dreadlocks, she was sort of attractive in a New Age-y kind of way. "I'm doing this to help Anita find her true path. She's blocked from it somehow. Find the lost dream, and she'll be back on track."

"'Tell me not in mournful numbers, life is but a dream,'" I began. "'For the—'"

"'Soul is dead that slumbers, and things are not as they seem,'" Madame Geri finished the quote. "Longfellow. Not my favorite poet, but he'll do in a pinch."

I blinked in surprise. "You like poetry?"

She didn't answer, merely picked up her leather tote bag and repositioned Marley on her shoulder. As she swept past me, I caught the scent of lavender. Surprisingly soft and subtle. I expected her to be wearing one of those patchouli perfumes that clung like the sickening, overpowering scent of something buried in a bog for a couple of centuries.

"Oh, I almost forgot: The boy you seek is missing,

but not in the way you think," she murmured under her breath to me.

"What did you say?" I caught her elbow. Marley squawked and raised his wings. Inside the green feathers appeared red and bluish markings. I instantly drew back.

Madame Geri pivoted. "You heard me," she replied with a wink. Jimmy then escorted her out of the office, bag, bird, and all.

I remained rooted in my spot until Marley had safely exited the office.

"Criminy." I dropped into my desk chair, not sure if I should break out a lucky rabbit's foot or say a prayer. "Is she a piece of work, or what?"

Sandy folded her arms across her ample chest, her face tightening in disapproval. "Be careful. Madame Geri is well respected on Coral Island."

"Sandy, her newspaper column is ridiculous. All she ever says is stuff like, 'Organize your thoughts, and you'll have a productive day.' Who can't forecast that?"

Sandy looked affronted. "Madame Geri does more than just write a column for the paper. She gives Tarot card readings, does astrological charts, and makes predictions about the future."

"I hate to ask this, but have any of them come true?"

Sandy nodded with a vigorous jerk of her head. "She predicted the early-season tropical storm last summer."

"I don't remember that."

"That's 'cause she made the prediction before you

came to the island. We were all prepared because Madame Geri told us about the storm in April. Then, when it hit in June, when you had moved here, no one panicked. We knew it was coming."

"I think I'll stick with the weather channel."

"Suit yourself." Sandy shrugged. "Believe it or not, Madame Geri *is* psychic."

Not. "Then again, she did say something sort of odd to me when she left about a missing boy." I laughed at my own foolishness. I knew better. Not because I doubted Madame Geri, but because one of my previous jobs had been with a psychic hotline. Okay, I'm not proud of it. I did it only for a couple of months. Mostly I listened to callers who wanted to talk about boyfriends who never called back, kids who called their friends constantly, or parents who couldn't remember to call. People just wanted to talk—to anyone. But they already knew the answers. I was no more of a psychic than Sandy was a voodoo queen. Still . . . how did Madame Geri know about Kevin? "Chances are, Wanda Sue told Madame Geri that she was worried about her grandson."

"Is something wrong with Kevin?"

"I'm not sure. His dad picked him up from school yesterday, and they never showed at Sally Jo's house. Nor was Kevin at school today." I rooted around in my canvas bag for my Official Reporter's Notepad. "Everyone seems to think they took off for a fishing trip. . . ."

"They've done it before. Tom lives to fish, and Kevin loves it too, from what I've heard."

"Yeah, you're probably right." I turned on my computer. I had more important things to concentrate on right now. Like finishing the Town Hall story and finding an angle on a jump rope marathon that would make it worthy of front-page reportage. I sighed and started flipping through my notes.

I finished both stories by late afternoon. Luckily, Anita hadn't returned, so I could make my escape before she had the chance to do her usual hatchet job.

I set hard copies of "Town Hall Meeting Approves Park Equipment" (the title didn't thrill me, either) and "Island Hoppers" (a little more creative) on her desk. Needless to say, neither story was Pulitzer Prize material. But Pulitzer never lived on little ol' Coral Island either.

Sandy had already left to get a cup of coffee with Jimmy, so I locked the office door behind me.

Slipping into my Windbreaker, I hurried toward my truck. While I was en route to my rust bucket, a shiny black Ford F-150 pulled up behind it.

The driver's window rolled down with a smoothness that screamed "automatic power." I tried not to drool with envy.

Detective Billie poked his head out. "I wanted to let you know that I questioned some of the guys at the Trade Winds Marina. They told me that Tom took his boat out late yesterday and said he was taking Kevin fishing."

"So they didn't disappear after all." I wrapped my arms around me in a vain attempt to keep the chilly wind from sapping away my body heat.

"Nope."

"Did any of the other fishermen hear where Tom was going? I'm sure Sally Jo would like to know."

"Little Coral Pass."

My teeth began to chatter. "Do you want me to tell Wanda Sue?"

He nodded. "I'll stop by Sally Jo's house and let her know."

"She'll appreciate that." Something tugged at the back of my mind; the whole "fishing trip" thing didn't feel right. "But—"

"Don't you own a decent coat?"

"This is Florida." I hiked up the collar of my Windbreaker. "I not supposed to need a coat."

He laughed—a rich, throaty sound that made my toes curl. "You'll need that and more if this cold snap keeps up."

"Oh, no. You mean it could get even cooler?" I rubbed my hands together. I didn't own a pair of gloves either.

"Maybe down to freezing." His glance locked on my curls, and his mouth turned up slightly on one side. "I might have to warm myself on your hair."

"Thanks a lot." *Sue me, a spark ignited inside me.*

"Anytime. See ya." He drove off, a sleek, dark man in his equally sleek, dark truck. *Wow.* I had to take a couple of deep breaths and force my heartbeat to re-sume its normal rhythm. For once he had sought me out to give me information, but I needed to play it cool and not badger him. That meant, most certainly, I needed to restrain myself from running after his truck to express my doubts. But going off half-cocked was my specialty.

Maybe I should get Madame Geri to do an astrologi-cal chart for me. Then I could figure out why I always seemed to sabotage things when they were going well.

Another arctic blast drove all philosophical musings right out of my mind. I hopped into Rusty and cranked up the heat. As the warmth penetrated my body, I vowed that I wouldn't ruin the good thing I had going here on Coral Island by always looking for trouble and pushing the island cop for more information. I had a de-cent job, a tiny but regular paycheck, and a place to call home—sort of. I couldn't blow it.

A short while later I drove to Mango Bay and turned in at the Twin Palms RV Resort. I slowed down to the requi-site 15 mph and glanced around for any sign of Wanda Sue. But she was nowhere to be seen. Like the rest of the islanders, she was probably indoors huddled under a quilt and drinking hot chocolate until the thermometer edged back up to seventy degrees.

A couple of new, massive Class A RVs occupied sites close to mine. It wasn't quite tourist season yet, but a steady stream of RVs had been checking in over the last three weeks. Even though it felt bitterly cold to me, I realized this was nothing compared to temperatures in Michigan or Ohio, which is where most of the seasonal residents came from. They'd be out in their shorts and T-shirts getting windburn—just to show the folks back home their faux tan.

As I parked Rusty, my glance strayed to the Wanderlodge next door. Sealed tight, the window treatments effectively shielded the mystery guests inside from my inquisitive, prying eyes. I scanned it for any further clues. Nada.

Maybe that in itself was a clue. The couple inside that behemoth on wheels was *so* famous, they didn't want to give even the slightest hint of their identity.

Jennifer Lopez and Marc Anthony? Maybe that jazz music I'd heard the previous day was designed to throw me off track.

Could it be?

I slid out of my truck, keeping my eyes on the Wanderlodge. J. Lo was a singer and often traveled in a plush motor home. *A definite possibility.*

Letting myself into the Airstream, I reached down and scooped up Kong. "Did you miss me today?"

He licked my face.

"I'll take that as a yes."

I sighed as Kong continued to lick my face. I might not have a male companion in my life right now, but I had unconditional, unbridled canine love.

"I know you need a walk, but let me check my messages first." The light was blinking on my answering machine.

I pressed the rewind button.

"Mallie, call me as soon as you get in," Wanda Sue's twang rang out with urgency.

I reached for the phone, but at that moment someone banged on the door of my Airstream.

"Mallie, Mallie!" Wanda Sue shouted.

Clutching Kong, I swung the door open.

Her eyes appeared wild and frantic. "The guys at the marina heard from Kevin—he's out on his daddy's boat, and Tom is missing. Kevin is all alone out there, and I'm afraid something will happen to him. Help me, honey. You've just got to help me!" She burst into tears.

Chapter Five

"Wanda Sue, try to stay calm." Not sure how to help, I patted her arm.

"If anything happens to that boy, I don't know what I'll do. He's my only grandson and just the sweetest little guy you'd ever imagine." She shook her head, swiping at the tears with a white cotton handkerchief. "He's never given his family a day's trouble in his whole life, and now this. . . ."

"Did you call Nick Billie?" I refrained from mentioning what I'd heard about Kevin's alleged petty crimes. Now wasn't the time. Besides, my info was only a rumor passed on by a sullen, jump-rope–hating kid with an even more sullen, rude father. It was always possible that Kevin might, in fact, be the golden boy Wanda Sue thought he was.

57

"Nick is on his way to the Trade Winds Marina right now. I know he can handle things, but it's gonna be dark soon, and I'm just plumb half out of my mind with worry for my grandson."

"What can I do?"

"Could you drive me to the marina? I don't think I could get behind the wheel right now, and I need to hear Kevin's voice."

"Sure. Let me give Kong a nanosecond walk, and I'll be ready to roll." Kong's little bladder would burst if I didn't attend to him.

"Thanks, Mallie." Wanda Sue dabbed at her eyes again, mascara coming off in big clumps. "I'm just a basket case right now."

I grabbed Kong's leash and shuttled him to the areca palm across from my RV site. He merely sniffed the tree. "Come on, Kong. This is your favorite spot. Do something. Quick."

He looked up at me. Nothing happened.

"All right, have it your way. But I'm going to put you in the truck, so we can finish this later." I scooped him up in my arms and strode toward Rusty. "Wanda Sue, you're going to have to hold Kong."

"Why, sure, honey."

I deposited him in Wanda Sue's arms. He started to whine, but I silenced him with a stern look.

In a few minutes all three of us were speeding down Cypress Road, heading for the marina. "Did Kevin say anything about his dad's disappearance?"

"Not really. They told me he sounded so scared, he didn't seem to know what he was saying." Her voice quavered. "He just wants to come home."

"Don't worry—he will."

"I hope so." Fear laced her voice.

"If there's one person I'd trust to bring him home safely, it's Nick Billie. He won't rest till he's made sure that Kevin is all right."

"I know that. It's just so . . . so hard to imagine my grandson out there in the Gulf all by his lonesome. He's only ten years old. Barely old enough to bait his own fishing pole."

"But he figured out how to work the radio, so he's not completely helpless," I pointed out.

Wanda Sue contemplated that for a few moments, nuzzling the top of Kong's head. "You're right. He's a smart boy. He won't do anything foolish."

I reached over and squeezed her hand. We drove the rest of the way in silence, except for the sound of Kong's staccato breathing. For a tiny dust mop, he could vie with his larger canine brothers when it came to heavy breathing.

At the island center, we turned onto Coral Island Road—the lone exit that led off the island—and headed for Paradisio, where the Trade Winds Marina was located. A fishing village that separated the island from the mainland, Paradisio wasn't much more than a smattering of bait shops, T-shirt/flip-flop stores, and fresh fish markets.

As we pulled up to the marina, I pointed at the black Ford F-150. "There's Detective Billie's truck."

We climbed out of Rusty and headed for the main office. She passed Kong to me as if he were a football and I was headed for a touchdown. Kong tucked his head under my armpit, and I charged forward with Wanda Sue.

She flung open the door to the marina office. "How's Kevin? Are you still talking to him? What are you going to do? Is he—"

"Wanda Sue, take it easy." Detective Billie rose from his position near the two-way radio. He moved toward her and placed an arm around her shoulders. "Kevin is all right. The boat is anchored—all safe and sound at Little Coral Pass. I radioed the Coast Guard to tell them we're going to take a trawler out there to pick him up." He spoke in a calm, reassuring tone. "Right now he's still on the radio. You can talk to him, but you've got to pull yourself together. Kevin needs you to be strong."

She took in a deep breath and nodded. "I'm okay."

"That's the spirit." He led her to the marine radio. "Just keep him talking. It'll give him something to focus on." He showed her how to use the radio.

Wanda Sue looked at it for a long moment. Then she clicked it on. "Kevin? This is your nana. How ya doing, sonny?"

"I'm okay." A boy's voice came through the static. "I . . . I miss you."

"I know. But you'll be back here in two shakes of a lamb's tail."

"Promise?"

"I promise. Nick Billie is going out there to pick you up. So all you need to do is sit tight and wait."

"Okay. But I'm cold, nana."

"I know. Bundle up with blankets."

Detective Billie motioned me to a corner. "Thanks for bringing her. It's just what Kevin needs." His dark eyes fastened on me with approval. "I couldn't get hold of Sally Jo."

"Just trying to help." Could my legs keep me upright if he continued to look at me like that?

"I see you brought some backup." He rubbed between Kong's ears.

Kong peeked at him. Much to my embarrassment, shameless teacup poodle that he is, Kong nuzzled Detective Billie's hand.

"That's odd. He doesn't normally take to strangers. And he can be downright fierce when it comes to unfamiliar men."

"Maybe he's having a change of heart." I could swear Detective Billie's voice had lowered to a husky murmur.

"I guess that can happen." What was he saying? Whose heart was changing? The dog's? His? Maybe I did need Madame Geri—pronto. My radar was askew right now.

He opened his mouth to say something else, but at that moment Pete Cresswell blew in.

"Hi ya, Mallie." He gave me quick hug, careful not to crush Kong.

"Hi, yourself." I grinned. Pete was the local fisher-man who'd been accused of murder last summer. My finding the real killer had gotten him off the hook, and since then he and his wife, Nora, had been beyond grateful as they put their lives back together. Pete was managing the marina, and Nora worked part-time at the Seafood Shanty. Needless to say, they'd become good friends of mine.

"We've got the marina's cabin cruiser all gassed up and ready to go," Pete said.

"Thanks, pal," Detective Billie replied.

Pete tried to stroke Kong. He growled. That was more like the Kong I knew and loved.

"You want me to go with you?" Pete asked Nick.

"No, I need you here to handle the radio and keep try-ing Sally Jo's number." Detective Billie turned to me. "I know this is asking a lot, but could you come along? Wanda Sue gets deathly seasick, and I think a woman's touch might help when we pick up Kevin."

"Me?" My first reaction was shock. Then a new and unexpected warmth surged through me.

"If you think you're up to it." He paused. "You don't get seasick, do you?"

"No, never." Actually, I had no idea if I'd get seasick or not. I'd never been on a boat, except the Pirates of the Caribbean ride at Disney World. And I didn't think that counted, because it was a small craft on a mechanically-run water track in a climate-controlled, totally artificial lagoon. "I'm sure I'll be fine."

"Okay, let's get going. I want to reach Kevin before sunset."

"Mallie, please bring my grandson back to me!" Wanda Sue exclaimed.

I gave her a thumbs-up and deposited Kong into her arms. "Have somebody take him for a walk soon."

"Will do." Pete handed me a Thermos and a small paper bag. "Nora sent these over for Kevin. It's hot tea and homemade oatmeal cookies."

I flashed him a brief smile of thanks, then followed Detective Billie out of the office. We hurried toward the docks.

"Looks like the wind has dropped, thank goodness. Not much of a chop on the water." He looked out over the small bay. "We should be able to make it out to the pass in about thirty minutes."

I trailed him with steps that began to slow the closer I came to the docks. What had possessed me to agree to this rescue mission? I didn't know a chop from a wave. And I certainly didn't know anything about boats. I swallowed hard. *Keep it together—for Wanda Sue.*

We halted in front of a newish-looking, midsized boat with a small cabin. Painted white with a green strip along the bottom part, it looked well cared for and seaworthy to my untrained eye. At least it probably wouldn't sink anytime soon.

Detective Billie jumped onto the deck with an easy grace. I stood rooted on the dock.

"Come on." He motioned me on board.

"Uh . . . maybe this wasn't such a good idea." I eyed the eight-inch space between the dock and the side of the boat. What if I missed and fell in? I might get hypothermia and—

All of a sudden, two strong arms clamped around my waist and lifted me into the boat.

"I don't have time to deal with indecision right now. Either you're going with me, or I can put you back on the dock. What's it to be?" Nick Billie looked down at me.

"I'm going." *Please don't let me be seasick,* I chanted silently. *If Wanda Sue's grandson could survive out there all by himself, the least I can do is help rescue him without barfing.*

Detective Billie cranked the engine. It sputtered a few times, then roared to life. "Undo the line!" he shouted.

I untied the rope connecting the boat to the dock and, before I could think, threw the entire thing onto the dock. *Oops.*

He revved the engine a few times, shifted the boat into gear, and moved away from the dock. "Okay?"

"Okay." I joined him under the covered part of the boat where the wheel and engine throttle were located. No need to tell him I'd thrown off the wrong end of the rope.

He zipped up his fleece-lined black leather jacket, then eyed my flimsy Windbreaker. "Are you going to be warm enough?"

"I've got on a flannel shirt under this and a T-shirt under that. It's called layering. Helps with the cold."

Actually, I don't know if it helped or not. But I didn't have the money to buy a real coat right now, so I had to improvise with arctic-coping strategies I'd seen on the Discovery Channel.

"Some weather for Florida, huh?" He cracked a smile.

"I didn't expect it, I can tell you that." I was tempted to move closer to him—to share body warmth, that's all. Purely for survival.

About twenty minutes passed, the boat slapping the water the only sound that pierced the silence between us. The sun dipped behind dense, sooty clouds that were turning the sky a dull, gunmetal gray. I shivered.

"We're almost at the pass." Detective Billie steered toward the far side of the bay. The boat arced in a half circle toward our target destination, and I gripped the side to steady myself.

"Why do you think Tom took his son out to fish in weather like this? That s-seems sort of dumb to me," I stammered, trying to let my body sway *with* the pitching of the boat, but the thumping motion of each wave caused me to stiffen.

"A lot of men on this island live to fish. Some are third or fourth generation fishermen. Unless there's a hurricane, they think it's okay to be out on the water."

"But with a kid?"

"They like to start 'em young."

I clucked my tongue. It seemed one step removed from those parents who'd throw their babies into the water and trust them to surface with an instinctive dog paddle. Heck, Kong could barely stand to put a paw in water, and he *was* a dog.

"Well, Detective Billie, what do you think happened to Tom?" I widened my stance on the deck, bending my knees slightly. *Please let us get to Kevin soon.*

"It's Nick, now that you're part of my crew." He smiled briefly; then his mouth tightened into a thin line as he straightened out the boat. "Sorry to say it, but Tom probably had too many beers and fell overboard. It's been known to happen."

Another shiver snaked through me like liquid lightning. "If he couldn't make it back on board his boat, then he might have . . ." I didn't want to say the word.

"Drowned." His tone was flat, unemotional, but the grim set of his features told me he didn't hold out much hope. "There's the boat." He gestured toward a ramshackle vessel bobbing up and down in the middle of a channel that separated two mangrove islands. "This is going to be tricky. I've got to get us around the stern of his boat, then drop anchor to the port side."

Stern? *Port*? I was lost.

He must have sensed my confusion. "Here, you take the wheel, and when I say so, cut back on the speed with the throttle." He pointed at the stick with a round knob at the end. "Shift it to neutral."

I took his place, and he moved to the front of the boat. Then he exclaimed, "Where's the line?"

"I . . . I sort of threw it overboard back at the dock."

He cursed in a language I didn't understand, in all

likelihood Miccosukee. But I didn't need a translation to get the gist of it.

We drew closer to the other boat. I could see a little boy standing on the back deck, his face panic-stricken as he waved his arms up and down.

"Everything's going to be all right, Kevin. Just stay put!" Nick shouted. "We're going to come up alongside you."

The boy settled down.

"Okay, ease back on the throttle," he said to me.

I jerked it downward, and the engine cut out immediately.

"I didn't mean shut it *down*. I meant *neutral*!" He darted to the edge of the boat. "Try to steer us toward Kevin. We should drift in that direction."

I did my best, yanking the wheel, and luckily the water seemed to push us in Kevin's direction.

"Kevin, throw me a line," Nick instructed.

The boy grabbed a thick rope and tossed it to him. Nick caught it and tied it around the metal thingamajig on our vessel. In spite of his fast work, our boat still slammed into the other boat, knocking Nick sideways. He quickly recovered and stretched out a hand to the boy.

"Don't be afraid. I won't let go of you."

The boy extended five shaking fingers. The boats rammed each other again, but somehow Nick managed to grasp Kevin's hand and hold on. Then he hoisted the boy onto our boat.

"Way to go!" I enthused.

Our intrepid island cop carried Kevin under the canopy, where I was. *Wow.*

"What happened to your dad?" Nick asked, setting Kevin down and rubbing his hands up and down the boy's arms to warm him.

"I don't know. Like I told you on the radio, I woke up, and he was gone." Kevin's teeth chattered as he tried to blink back the tears.

"Okay. We'll talk later." He gave the boy a brief hug. "This is Miss Mallie. She's going to take care of you while I get us home, okay?"

Kevin managed to wag his head, his face pinched with cold.

"I'll take him below." I put an arm around his thin shoulders. "I've got some hot tea and Nora Cresswell's yummy oatmeal cookies. Would you like some?"

His teeth chattered around something that sounded like a yes.

"You two go ahead. I need to stabilize the boat and check out the area." Detective Billie grabbed a pair of binoculars.

I led Kevin down the stairs into the small cabin. It held a mini kitchen, a table with two cushioned seats, and a pair of bunks in the front, which tapered to a point. Neat and tidy with the smell of leather dipped in seawater. *Nice.*

Wrapping a thick wool blanket around Kevin, I settled him on the seat next to the table. Then I filled a mug with the steaming liquid and handed it to him.

"Thanks, miss." He gulped down the hot tea.

"You can call me Mallie." I took in his short brown hair, soft blue eyes, and sensitive features. I had never met Sally Jo, but if she looked anything like Wanda Sue, Kevin must resemble his dad.

"Is that better?" I sat next to him, slipping an arm around his quaking shoulders.

"Uh-huh. Could I have some more?" He held out the mug.

"Sure." I smiled and reached for the Thermos.

As I refilled his mug, I heard muffled swearing from on deck—this time in English.

"You stay here, Kevin." I scrambled up the stairs and moved toward the back of the boat, where Detective Billie stood very still, head lowered. "What's up?"

He handed me the binoculars and pointed to the mangroves off in the distance. I held the glasses up to my eyes. For an instant I couldn't see anything as my vision adjusted to the lenses. Then I spotted it—a man's body flung against the clawlike mangrove roots.

"Tom?" I mouthed without speaking.

He nodded.

Chapter Six

I stayed belowdecks for the choppy trip back to the
Trade Winds Marina, keeping Kevin distracted so he
wouldn't hear Detective Billie radio the Coast Guard to
pick up his father's body. We talked about school, his
favorite band—the Jonas Brothers—the latest Harry Pot-
ter movie, and what kind of fish he liked to eat.

Coming up with topics proved surprisingly easy,
considering I wasn't used to kids. Didn't have any and
didn't know anyone who did. The world of car pools,
after-school activities, and kiddie films was unknown
to me—if you discounted my brief sojourn at Disney
World, which I tried to do. Those multitudes of Mickey
Mouse worshippers seemed like aliens from another
planet. Not that there was anything wrong with them;
I just didn't connect.

But sitting with Kevin in the cozy confines of the boat cabin, I had my first upfront, close, and personal contact with a kid. It wasn't half bad. Even if some of his schoolmates called him a juvenile delinquent, he'd just lost his father, and I found myself welling up with a sudden, unexpected maternal desire to protect him.

A strange reaction but not unpleasant. *Not at all.*

"Mallie, I need your help!" Detective Billie shouted from above.

"Stay here where it's warm." I squeezed Kevin's arm in reassurance.

"Okay." He turned his attention to the plate of oatmeal cookies I'd set down next to the hot tea.

I emerged from the cabin and realized the weather had worsened. A cold, hard rain now fell, and the bay waters churned with small whitecaps, the boat thumping hard on the surface. Somehow Detective Billie, standing at the wheel with his features set in a determined expression, kept the boat chugging in a steady path toward the marina. His hair plastered to his head, hands gripping the wheel, he seemed more than a match for whatever the elements could throw his way.

My heart beat a little faster.

"How's Kevin?" He glanced briefly in my direction.

"Settling down a bit, but he's still dazed." I steadied myself by gripping the back of the captain's chair. "Don't you think it's odd that Tom went to all the trouble to take his son on a fishing trip, then drank too much and fell overboard?"

He groaned. "Don't start hypothesizing—it's not the time or place." Nick flashed me a warning glance. "There's no point in speculating before we know for sure what happened."

"I'm just thinking out loud." I watched the birds overhead struggle to fly against the wind, soaring upward, then dipping low, to find a clear path. "Guess I'm just nervous."

He nodded as he steered the boat toward the marina docks.

"Here—take the wheel." Nick stepped out of the way and positioned me in the captain's chair. "Look, I know this is a tough situation, but I need you to do as I say for once." He stood behind me, his hands on my shoulders. "I can't trust you to handle the line, but I don't want us to ram the dock either."

"Okay." I tried to push all thoughts of Tom's death out of my mind. *Focus.*

Detective Billie moved to the front of the boat. I throttled back the engine on his command, and when we drew close enough to the dock, he jumped off and retrieved the rope. He then tied up.

Every movement exhibited his muscular grace and economy of movement. Strong yet controlled. Intent on getting the job done and not making mistakes. That was Nick's credo—he didn't like to mess up—whereas I made a habit of regularly messing up. Except this time. Aside from the rope debacle, I'd handled myself pretty well on the boat.

Permitting myself a tiny smile of satisfaction, I cut off the engine and called down to Kevin. He came up on deck, his hands shoved into his jeans pockets.

"Is Mom here?" he asked.

"If Wanda Sue was able to call her—" Detective Billie began.

"Kevin!" a woman exclaimed as she came running toward the dock.

"Mom!" Kevin scrambled off the boat and torpedoed into a petite woman sporting a honey-colored, retro-sixties flip hairdo and candy-cane–pink warm-up suit. *Had to be Wanda Sue's daughter, all right.*

She wrapped her arms around him and nuzzled the top of his head with her face. "I was so worried about you," she said over and over.

I gulped hard, my eyes bordered with tears.

"Thanks a lot, Mallie." Nick now stood next to me.

"I came along for the ride." I shrugged, turning away, not wanting him to see how much I was affected by the touching scene. I was Mallie Monroe, flaky and carefree, totally unsentimental, not the type of person to start sobbing over a mother and son reuniting. I didn't let myself get involved like that. "It was nothing."

"Not to me—or them."

I didn't dare look at him. All my defenses were down, and that could be dangerous. The last time it happened was Valentine's Day in Orlando, after my boyfriend de jour had left to "find himself" out West. I ended up at my Airstream around 2:00 A.M. with a butterfly tattoo on my ankle and my hair dyed with electric blue streaks. Fortunately, the tattoo was a wash-off kind and the dye temporary. A lucky escape.

"Oh, there's Wanda Sue." I pointed to my landlady, closing in on her daughter and grandson. Without waiting for a reply, I jumped off the boat and headed toward them.

"How can Sally Jo and I ever thank you, Mallie?" Wanda Sue gushed as she gave me a long, hard hug.

"No need. I'm just happy that we were able to bring Kevin home all safe and sound." I smiled down at him.

"I'll be forever grateful," Sally Jo joined in. Her face was a younger version of Wanda Sue's, all right. Same wide mouth, snub nose, and over-plucked brows. "My son means everything to me."

"Detective Billie did all the work. I just . . . uh . . . threw him a rope."

"She did more than that," he said as he approached us, his hard-planed features softened for once. "Let's go inside. It's cold out here, and we need to talk."

"Where's Tom?" Sally Jo scanned Detective Billie's face. He didn't answer. She bit her lip and blinked several times, her eyes welling with tears.

Wanda Sue looked at me. I cast my glance downward.

Silently we trooped into the marina office, our silence telling them what they needed to know. Then Kong's excited yapping greeted me. I scooped him up and clutched him to my chest. He was the one constant in this crazy, sad day. My canine life preserver.

The rest of the evening passed in a blur. We huddled near the space heaters while Detective Billie took care of the arrangements for the Coast Guard to retrieve Tom's body. Eventually Kevin fell asleep in his mother's arms, and my head began to droop like a wilted flower. After the adrenaline rush of Kevin's rescue, exhaustion hit and drained the energy from my body.

"Why don't you go home?" Nick finally said to me. "There's nothing more you can do here. After Wanda Sue and Sally Jo identify the body, I'll take them home."

I turned to Wanda Sue. "You going to be okay?"

"We'll be just fine," she said, her hands trembling. "We got our boy back—that's something."

With leaden feet, I exited the marina office, still carrying Kong. What had started out as your average Coral Island morning had turned into a day fraught with a missing boy, miscast ropes, and a dead man. *Major bummer.*

I nuzzled the top of Kong's head. At least Kevin was safe. But, then again, his father was dead. And, in spite of my fatigue, I wanted to know what had happened.

The next morning, I awoke to the jangling of my faux leopard-skin Princess telephone. It had cost $19.95 at a discount store and had one of those cheap, shrill rings that sounded like squeaking brakes on a rain-slick road. But since I was still living from paycheck to paycheck, it would do just fine.

"Hello."

"Mallie, how are you? It's your mother."

Oh, no.

"Are you still in bed? What a sleepyhead."

I opened one eyelid to check the clock on my night-stand. "Oh, yeah. It's almost six-thirty. The day is prac-tically over." Kong licked the side of my face, as if to reassure me. I held the phone up so he could listen.

My mom laughed with a high-pitched twitter. "Your sister, Paula, is always up with the dawn to jog before she goes to work. Honestly, I don't know how she does it. A full-time job, two kids, and a husband who's a doc-tor. She's remarkable."

I silently mouthed the last two words with her, hav-ing heard them a hundred times before.

"We spoke to your great-aunt last night, and she said you were doing very well in your little newspaper job." She paused.

"You could say that." *Translated: We're amazed you've kept this job longer than six months.*

"Keep up the good work, Mallie."

"Thanks." *Translated: We don't think you'll last an-other six months."*

She cleared her throat. *Translated: I'm about to drop a bomb.*

"Your father and I . . . uh . . . were thinking about vis-iting you on Coral Island."

I jerked into an upright position, knocking Kong onto the floor; he whined in protest. "Oops, sorry." I whisked him up into my arms and hugged him.

"Sorry about what?"

"Nothing—I was talking to Kong."

"Oh . . . well, anyway, we want to visit Coral Island. Maybe check it out along with some other Florida locales." Her tone was so abnormally chipper, it almost caused sunshine to spill out of the receiver. I looked around in vain for my sunglasses. "Your father and I are thinking about buying a retirement home. Nothing big, mind you. Maybe a four thousand square foot cottage with a swimming pool, cabana, and tennis court— somewhere on the water with a country club nearby. The kind of place where we can be part of a community of like-minded people."

I gasped. *My parents on Coral Island? With no buffer?* "I . . . I thought you hated Florida. Said it was full of bugs and displaced crazies."

"All the more reason for people like us to move there—we're dependable, solid, cultured. Just imagine how much we could improve the tone of life. And the warm winters would be nice."

"It does get cold here," I felt obligated to point out. "Almost frigid at times."

"Really?"

"Oh, yes."

Silence. *Translated: I know you're lying, but I'll just pass over that for now and wound you very deeply later.*

"It doesn't matter, Mallie. We still want to visit." Her tone was firm, final.

Kong hid his head under my pillow. I wanted to do

the same. "All right. Let me know when you're coming," I managed to get out between clenched teeth.

"It may be sooner than you think."

Uh-oh.

"Look for us when you see us. Ta-ta." She hung up.

Ta-ta? I stared at the phone, then fell back onto my bed in defeat.

It took me three donuts and two twelve-ounce black coffees to get my equilibrium back after the phone conversation with my mother. *Not to mention the "Ta-ta." Where did that come from?*

By the time I breezed into the *Observer* office, I was able to suppress the dread over her possible visit and even manage what I thought passed for a cheery greeting to Sandy.

"Did your mother call this morning?" she inquired after one look at my face.

"Does it show?"

Her eyes grew openly amused. "You get this trapped-animal look, and your lips freeze up."

I flexed the corners of my mouth up and down to get them to relax again, but the whole lower half of my face felt as stiff as cement.

"You need to talk to *my* mom," Jimmy the Painter chimed in. Dressed in his white, paint-splattered overalls, he was perched on the side of Sandy's desk, apparently taking a water break. "She specializes in family problems. Helps you to clear the negative energy."

"I appreciate the offer. But I think I'll do it the old-fashioned way—bury my anger in work and then kick the dog when I get home."

Jimmy looked so taken aback, I hastened to assure him that I was joking. I'd never take so much as a pinkie toe to Kong.

"We heard about what happened last night," Sandy said, tucking the price tag into the sleeve of her soft beige angora sweater. "Too bad about Tom. He was a good guy."

My mind went back to the scene yesterday, when I saw Tom's body splayed against the mangroves. I shuddered inwardly.

"Detective Billie thinks he was probably drinking too much, fell overboard, and drowned." I sat down at my desk and flipped through my notes. "What do you think?"

Sandy tapped her chin. "It's possible. Tom liked his beer, but so does every other red-blooded guy on this island."

"Not me," Jimmy said, holding up a bottled water with a wink.

"You're special." Sandy flashed a smile at him, one of those soft, feminine, I'm-stuck-on-you, intimate-as-a-kiss smiles. Good for her. At least one of us had a decent male prospect.

"Tom would've had to drink an awful lot to fall overboard," I pointed out.

"True." Sandy turned her attention back to me. "And I don't think he was the type to drink that much when he had his son on the boat. Tom was a good father. He loved Kevin a lot."

My eyes met hers. "If it wasn't an accident, that means someone deliberately knocked him overboard."

"But who?"

"I don't know. Kevin was the only other person on the boat. . . ."

We stared at each other for a few moments, unable to say the words aloud.

"It's time to get Mom on it." Jimmy stood up and shook out his tattered overalls. "She'll be able to tell if there was foul play."

"Give her a call, Mallie," Sandy urged. "Oh, and tell her to hurry up with Anita's astrological chart while you're at it."

"I just might." *Hah.*

"Might what?" Anita asked as she breezed into the office, chomping on her gum with loud smacks.

"Uh . . . I might take an early lunch," I lied.

"Nobody is going to lunch today when we've got a dead body waiting to make the front page." Anita cackled, or it might've been a cough. I couldn't tell; it hadn't been all that long since she stopped smoking, and her lungs no doubt still contained soot the consistency of old asphalt. "By the by, nice move last night, Mallie. Making sure you were on the boat that rescued Kevin. Got some firsthand coverage there. *And* you were there to see his father's body—even better."

"I didn't plan it that way. Nick Billie asked me to go with him, and I did."

"Pffft." She waved a bony hand. "You're a reporter now. Anytime something happens, you have to think about how you're going to get the story. That's the important thing. If you pass an accident, slow down and check it out. If you see a bank robbery, chase down the culprit and interview him. If you see a body—"

"Call the police?" I offered.

"Take pictures." Anita motioned for me to follow her into her office.

Groaning inwardly, I rose to my feet and grabbed my notepad. Sandy gave me an encouraging smile as I trailed Anita into her glass-encased cubicle.

"Close the door," she ordered as she tossed her coat over the top of a battered file cabinet.

I complied, eying the gum wrappers littering the floor and hoping yet again that I wasn't stepping on anything gooey.

"Okay, what happened last night?" She folded her arms across her chest. Wearing a faded olive sweater and plaid polyester pants, she competed with me for the Cheapest Clothing To Keep Warm Award. "Did you get interviews?"

"Not really. But I did jot down some general notes." I held up my notepad.

"That's something, I guess. Let me see." She snatched it from my unresisting fingers and flipped through the pages. "This is a start. You can write about Kevin's rescue—that's got real human interest. Local boy and everything. Talk to his mother—she lives at Heron's Landing."

"What about finding Tom's body?" I eased into the plastic chair across from Anita's desk.

"That's your lead, kiddo. Knocks those mediocre Town Hall and Autumn Festival stories to page two. Death is big news. If you finish it by tomorrow, we'll make the Friday deadline for next week's edition." Anita tossed my notepad onto her desk. "Then you can do a follow-up story this weekend. By that time, cause of death should be determined, and we'll know if there was foul play."

"Detective Billie thinks that Tom got drunk and fell off the boat. Then he probably drowned." I ignored her criticism of my writing topics. Could I help it that not much happened on Coral Island that was particularly newsworthy?

"My instincts tell me that's off base."

"How so?"

"For one thing, the weather was miserable, the water choppy. Tom would've been extra careful when taking his son out in those conditions. And even if he did have a few beers, I can't see his being so drunk that he'd fall out of the boat. Tom grew up on boats. He could anchor or dock 'em in his sleep." She looked at me, her features growing amused. "Which is more than I can say about you from what I heard this morning. Did you actually throw the bow line off the boat?"

"I might have." Heat rose into my face, and I shifted in my chair. Well, it was official: The entire island knew about my boating ineptitude.

She guffawed—a rough, raspy sound. "You've got a lot to learn, kiddo."

"I'm trying."

She folded her arms across her bony chest. "Well . . . get to work."

I nodded, my embarrassment turning to annoyance as I exited Anita's office. Would it kill her to give me a word of praise or encouragement now and again? Sure, I was a rookie when it came to news, but I was developing a reporter's instinct. Sort of.

Sandy threw me a sympathetic look as I trudged toward my desk. "Hang in there, Mallie. We'll get that astrological chart done and figure out how to make Anita a human being."

"Fat chance." I turned on my old Dell desktop computer that I shared with Sandy. First, I checked my e-mails. One by one, I opened them. Nothing special. Just a couple of press releases from the elementary school about the upcoming Autumn Festival events. I yawned. Then I noticed that the last e-mail was from an unfamiliar name: *Salty Surfer.*

Huh?

I clicked on the message, and the words jumped out at me.

You're an outsider. Don't mess with things that ain't your business.

I blinked as I read it again. "Sandy, look at this." I swung the computer screen in her direction.

She gasped. "Is that some kind of joke?"

"If it is, it's in bad taste. Not to mention the poor grammar . . ."

Jimmy set down his paintbrush and joined us. He read the e-mail and let out a long, low whistle. "Heavy stuff."

"I'll say," I said. "It's probably just another disgruntled reader or something. Anita told me she gets them all the time. But who the heck would call himself Salty Surfer?"

"It's local jargon for a fisherman." Sandy's eyes clouded with uneasiness.

"Speaking of local fishermen, I had an unpleasant confrontation with Jake Fowler yesterday at the elementary school. He was angry because I'd interviewed his son, Robby, for my story."

"Stay away from him," Sandy said. "He's trouble."

"What's his problem?" I hit the Print button on the computer.

Sandy leaned forward in a conspiratorial manner. "His wife left him two years ago. He kept Robby but has been bitter ever since. Then he started a clam farm with Tom Crawford that went bankrupt. He blamed Tom— said he'd mismanaged the books and—"

"Jake Fowler hated Tom Crawford?" My interest spiked a couple of notches. "Enough to kill him?"

She shrugged. "I . . . I can't say for sure."

"If Tom were murdered, Jake would certainly have a motive," I murmured, half to myself. "A big one."

Silence fell over the newsroom, except for the muted coughs emanating from Anita's office cubicle.

"Don't worry." Jimmy placed a hand on Sandy's shoulder, then turned to me. "If you call Mom, she'll help."

"Thanks." I tried to summon a degree of enthusiasm, knowing full well I had no intention of putting myself in the hands of some half-baked, phony, island fortune-teller. I could get to the truth on my own. In spite of what Anita thought, I knew how to follow up on leads.

I grabbed my printout, shoved it into my canvas bag, and left.

Chapter Seven

In spite of Anita's suggestion that I skip lunch, I
swung by the Circle K and picked up yet another ham
and Swiss hoagie with a Coke (regular, not diet) to eat
on the road. As I took a couple of swigs of my drink, I
made for Heron's Landing—a tiny mobile-home community not far from the island center. A few of the local
fishing families lived there, including Sally Jo—my
first lead.

Nestled among the pine trees and mini citrus groves
stood a smattering of trailers firmly affixed to permanent sites. They weren't luxurious by any means, but,
freshly painted and landscaped with lots of native veg-
etation, they represented proudly the modest but hard-
working lifestyle of the local fishermen. Canals stretched
behind them so the men could dock their boats in the

backyard and deposit their "island Reeboks" on the back porch.

I looked for Wanda Sue's ancient, powder blue Cadillac convertible with its vanity plate—HOTTIE—no deep psychological delving needed there. It stood parked in front of a double-wide mobile home painted the color of a wild flamingo and trimmed with butterscotch yellow shutters.

My own silver Airstream with its black and white striped awning seemed tame in comparison.

I hopped out of Rusty and staggered against the wind gusts. Before I got within thirty feet of the front door, it swung open, and Wanda Sue poked her head out.

"Honey, we were just talking about you. Come on in before you freeze your buns off."

I didn't know if my behind would actually disconnect from my body, but it felt as if it was getting close to doing so.

As soon as I crossed the threshold, I welcomed the blast of heat. One thing about mobile homes—they might be small, but they had furnaces that could heat up the North Pole and then some.

"How 'bout a nice cup of hot cocoa?" Wanda Sue asked as she closed the door behind me. In spite of her cheery tone, the red-rimmed eyes told me she'd been crying.

"Love some."

I started to unzip my Windbreaker but halted as I took in my surroundings. Sally Jo's interior decorating taste ran somewhere between overstuffed Victorian and Southwest kitsch. A huge pink leather sectional dominated the living room, offset by glass end tables and matching coffee table with bases made of carved wooden horses. Rodeo pictures adorned every wall, illuminated by lamps with pink-fringed shades. A deep rose shag carpet completed the décor.

My mouth dropped open.

"It's really something, huh, Mallie? Can you believe that Sally Jo fixed this place up all by herself?"

"Uh . . . yeah." I had the urge to reach for some Maalox.

"She was all set to get her AA degree in interior design, but then she . . . got married . . . and had Kevin. And now . . ." Tears slid down Wanda Sue's face, and she brushed them away with an impatient swipe of her hand. "I've got to stop this. It ain't doing Sally Jo any good. She needs me to be strong right now, and that's what I'm gonna be." She took in a determined breath.

"How's she doing?"

"Pretty much like you'd expect. Plumb near to crazy. She got her boy back last night but lost her man. It's a terrible thing to happen, just terrible." Wanda Sue lowered her head and closed her eyes for a few brief moments. "But Kevin's okay. . . . We have to keep reminding ourselves that some good came out of last night."

"Where is he?" I finished unzipping my Windbreaker.

"Asleep in his bedroom." She motioned down a narrow hallway. "Poor little thing was all tuckered out after the commotion—what with being left out on that boat all day and up most of the night. We decided to keep him home from school so he could rest."

"Good idea." I sat down on the leather sofa. Immediately it settled around me in all its squishy pastel glory. For a moment I had the sensation of sitting in a tub of margarine. "Is Sally Jo resting too?"

"I'm right here." She emerged from the hallway, wearing a fluffy mauve robe and matching slippers. She walked with slow, halting steps, her face drawn and tired. But, amazingly, her sixties flip hair helmet was intact. *Must be genetic.* "Thanks for coming over, Mallie."

"You just set yourself down, baby." Wanda Sue guided Sally Jo to the monstrous sofa, picking up a pink and white crocheted coverlet on the way. "I'm gonna fix Mallie a cup of cocoa. Would you like one too?"

"Sure." Her voice was devoid of emotion.

Wanda Sue tucked the coverlet around her daughter, then made her way to the kitchen.

"Can I do anything?" I asked.

Sally Jo leveled two sad eyes in my direction. "You already did. You saved my son. I'm so grateful for that."

"All I did was help Detective Billie. He's the one you should be grateful to. He saved Kevin."

A ghost of a smile touched her face. "You *both* did."

"Well . . . sort of." She probably hadn't heard about the rope incident. *Small mercy.*

"I couldn't believe it when they brought in Tom's body. I mean, he didn't look dead or anything. His eyes were closed, but he seemed like he was sleeping." She buried her face in her hands. "It's so unfair. We were getting back together—going to be a family again. And now it's all gone. We'll never have the chance. . . ." Her voice trailed off into a muffled jumble.

"You and Tom were definitely getting back together?" I asked gently.

She raised her head, her face streaked with tears. "We'd been separated for about eight months, but in the last few weeks we'd started talking again, working out our problems. That's why I don't understand any of this. Just when everything was looking up, Tom goes and takes Kevin out on his boat without telling me, worrying me something sick. Why would he do that?"

"I don't know."

"Oh, God. How could he be so stupid? Now Kevin don't have a daddy." A fresh stream of tears spilled over her cheeks. "What are we gonna do?"

My motormouth sputtered. "You . . . you've got Wanda Sue and lots of people here who'll help out. If there's one thing I've learned about Coral Island, it's a place where people look out for one another."

She shook her head violently. "But that won't bring back my Tom. He's gone forever."

I scooted across the sofa and put my arms around her. She cried hard, hot tears that dropped onto my shoulder, and her whole body quaked as the sobs ran through her. Never having provided anyone with the proverbial shoulder to cry on, I wasn't sure if I was doing it right. But I improvised as best I could, patting her on the back and murmuring some incoherent words. After a few minutes she settled down.

I eased away. "Let me get that hot cocoa. It'll make you feel better."

She pushed a stray hair back. "I'd like that."

I gave her another quick pat on the arm and made my way into the kitchen. Wanda Sue had set out three mugs and was in the process of heating milk in a saucepan.

"This is a plumb nightmare," she said, shaking her head. "I can't hardly take it all in. Looking at poor Tom's body last night, dead as a doornail. Who would've thought?"

"It must've been rough on all of you."

"Worst thing I've ever had to do—and that includes burying my own husband six years ago. Angina. We knew it was coming. But this was different. Tom was so young." Her chin began to quiver, but she held back the tears. "Nick had Sally Jo and Kevin stay inside the marina office, while I identified the body. But then Sally Jo came out—she wanted to see him. It's so sad. I wish . . . things could've worked out different for them, especially since Tom planned to move back in. . . ."

"I hate to pry, but did Nick Billie say when he'd know the cause of death?"

"In a day or two." She sniffed.

I handed her a Kleenex from the box on the counter.

"Wanda Sue, if for some reason the cause of death isn't an accident, that opens up the possibility that someone . . . well . . . could've hurt Tom." I picked over my words as if I were tiptoeing over jagged shells on the beach.

Her glance sharpened. "What are you saying?"

"Isn't it sort of unlikely that Tom just fell overboard?"

"Kevin was the only other person on the boat." Her voice dropped to a whisper.

"True. . . ." An idea that had been simmering in the back of my mind rippled to the surface. "Unless someone else came aboard the boat—someone who wanted to kill Tom."

Her eyes grew large and liquid. "You think?"

"It's possible." I raised my hands, palms open, then dropped them. "But this is all supposition. Detective Billie might be right—he thought Tom fell out of the boat after a couple of beers."

The milk bubbled as it came to a boil. Wanda Sue then removed the pan from the stove and poured the steaming liquid into the mugs. "I don't think so," she said in a quiet voice.

"Why not?"

"I didn't tell Nick last night, but Tom and Sally Jo have been going to AA. Neither of them have touched alcohol for the last four months."

Wanda Sue's words hung in the air like a sudden, dark fog. We looked at each other, but neither of us wanted to say the words. If an accidental death were looking more and more unlikely, Kevin would be the primary suspect.

She turned away and stirred the instant cocoa with vigorous strokes. Then she held out two mugs. "Help me find out what happened on that boat. Kevin's future could be at stake. We need you, Mallie."

"I'll try." I took the mugs from her and carried them into the living room.

By the time I arrived at my Tae Kwon Do class that night, I was regretting my hasty agreement to help Wanda Sue. As Kevin's doting grandmother, she couldn't conceive that the boy might be capable of harming his own father. But if he'd been troubled by his parents' separation, he might've attacked Tom in a fit of rage. Younger kids than he had done similar crimes, so it wasn't out of the realm of possibility.

I parked Rusty outside the fitness center and climbed out. The wind had died down as evening set in, but now a biting chill was blanketing the island. I hurried inside, clutching my tattered gym bag.

"Mallie, good to see you." Sam held out his right hand and bowed. I did the same, and we shook hands. It still felt weird to greet someone this way, but I tried my best to conform to Tae Kwon Do etiquette.

Several members of the class waved. The Jordan twins ignored me.

"I wasn't sure if you'd be here tonight after your recent adventure," he said.

I tossed my gym bag to the floor. "Which one? Helping to rescue Kevin or making a fool of myself by pitching the bow line overboard?"

He smiled gently. "You're too hard on yourself. Everyone admires how much courage it took for you to go out on those rough seas yesterday when you'd never been on a boat before."

"Thanks." I took a deep breath and unzipped my gym bag. I'd bought this item at my usual consignment shop, and, even though it wasn't too old, it had a perennial smell of sweaty socks.

I grabbed my white belt and closed the bag again before I had to exhale.

"Do they know how Tom died?" Sam asked.

"Not yet." I wound the belt around my waist twice and attempted the correct knot formation. After two tries, Sam stepped toward me and, in one deft motion, executed a perfect knot.

"We'll talk after class. For now, try to empty your mind of everything that happened during the day. Focus on what we're going to do tonight."

"Fat chance."

He adjusted his own black belt. "That's because you're not used to being in the present. Ruminating is pointless—and it causes you to age." He pointed at his bald head. "I used to have thick, lustrous hair."

I laughed as I scraped back my curls and fastened them with an elastic band. "But pointless ruminating is one of my specialties. I'm not called Mixed-up Mallie for nothing."

"You underestimate yourself."

"That's another one of my specialties." In spite of my distracted state, the hour flew by, and the next thing I knew, we were bowing out of class. I stayed after everyone had left—except the Jordan twins.

I needed to talk to Sam. I needed a big dose of his wisdom. At the very least, I needed a mild sip of intelligent encouragement.

"Nice job," Sam said as he wiped his face with a towel. "You'll be ready to test for your yellow tip soon."

A tiny flicker of delight lit inside of me. "You mean I'll actually get some color in my white belt?"

"Absolutely."

"I can hardly wait." I unwound my belt and tossed it into the gym bag, holding my breath for the short, stinky interval during which it was unzipped. "At least I'm making some kind of measurable progress in Tae Kwon Do."

Sam removed his belt, folding it with careful, deliberate motions. "And you're not elsewhere?"

"I've been at the newspaper for almost six months, and Anita still treats me like a cub reporter, checking every story and rewriting almost every sentence. Can you believe that?"

"She's a stickler for a well-written article."

"Actually, I think she likes to stick it to me, period."

He laughed. "For a comparative literature major, you're got some colorful expressions." He tilted his balding head back and regarded me with a speculative gaze. "What's really bothering you?"

"How is it that you know me so well after only a few months?"

"I pay attention." A brief smile flitted over his face. "And there's always the island grapevine to fill in the gaps."

"It's this whole thing with Kevin's dad. . . . I sort of promised Wanda Sue I'd help find out what happened to Tom. But I'm concerned that the truth might end up implicating Kevin, and that would devastate her." I pulled the elastic band out of my hair and fluffed my curls. "Wanda Sue is counting on me, and that's such a . . ."

"Huge responsibility?" Calm understanding shone from his gray eyes.

"Yes," I said in a rush of relief. "I've never been the kind of person others could count on. It always seemed so . . . confining to meet people's expectations. All my adult life I've only had myself to look out for—"

"And to let down."

"Huh?"

"It's simple, really. If you don't have to meet others' expectations, you also avoid their disappointment when you don't live up to their version of how you should behave. You keep the world at arm's length. No demands, no close ties. That's comfortable. But it's also lonely. At some point you need to allow people to depend on you."

"What if I mess up?"

"If they care about you, they'll understand."

I chewed on my lower lip. "I mess up a lot, Sam."

"Who doesn't?" He put a hand on my shoulder. "You've told me that you wanted to put down roots here, be a part of the island community. This is what it's all about. You've got to let people depend on you—and allow yourself to depend on them."

"It's scary."

"Of course." He dropped his hand. "It's unsettling—like when you first started Tae Kwon Do. Remember when you couldn't do even twenty jumping jacks without being winded? Now you can do fifty with only slight panting. That's how we grow and develop—a little at a time. You just need to steer clear of limber teenagers." He motioned with his head toward the Jordan sisters, who were competing with each other on who could do the highest jump kick. "They make you want to run and hide."

"You can say that again." I laughed. "What do you think the truth is behind Tom's death? From what I've been able to gather, the only enemy he had was Jake Fowler—his ex-business partner. Jake held Tom responsible for their bankrupt clam farm. Anita always says, 'Follow the money,' and in this instance, it may or may not be true."

He paused. "If he was murdered, and I say 'if,' there might be other reasons besides money."

"Such as?"

"Passion, lust, anger, jealousy, hatred." He swung his attention back to me. "They're all deep emotions— strong enough to cause a person to take another's life."

I swallowed hard. Those were the very emotions I'd spent most of my life avoiding. I kept things light in all my relationships, and I wasn't sure I wanted to delve that deeply into the darker regions of the human soul. Too murky.

"You've found out who hated Tom. Now find out who loved him. There might be motivation for murder in either."

Sam packed up his sparring gear and ushered the Jordan sisters and me out. After he locked up, we left the fitness center without exchanging another word. A clear, starry night had set in—the kind that promised even colder temperatures by morning, maybe even a hard freeze. I drove back to the Twin Palms at Mango Bay and was happy to be greeted by Kong at the door of my Airstream.

Things were so much easier with a dog, so much simpler. In fact, I preferred my teacup poodle to almost any person. I provided him with food, exercise, and love, and he was happy. Ours was a perfect relationship. So why did I want more?

The empty silence of my Airstream answered me.

Chapter Eight

The next morning I was awakened once again by the shrill ring of my cheapie deluxe telephone. I groaned as I fumbled for the receiver. *Two parental calls in two days? What had I done to deserve such cruel and unusual punishment?*

"Hello?" I drew out the last syllable to convey my irritation.

"This is Nick Billie."

My eyes flew open. *Yahoo!*

"Did I wake you?"

"Oh, no. I've been up for an hour." I peeped at my alarm clock: 7:00 A.M. It was theoretically possible that I could've been awake that early. Of course, if he knew me better, he'd realize the actual possibility of that happening was zilch. "I had to take Kong for his walk, make coffee, straighten up my Airstream. You know, morning is the most important time of day. I like to use it to plan my articles. That way, when I get to the *Observer,* I'm ready to hit the keyboard and run with it. Now, if I had a laptop here, I'd probably get even more done at home, but the newspaper isn't about to fork out that kind of money. Not with getting the office painted and—"

"Okay, okay. I get the picture," he cut in, impatience threaded through his voice.

I resisted the urge to place a pillow over my face and suffocate my motormouth. Why, oh, why did it always kick in at the most inopportune moments?

"I thought you might like to swing by the station on your way to work—that is, if you can interrupt your creative marathon."

"What's up?"

"I've got Tom's autopsy results."

"And you're willing to share them with me?" I sat up, glad he couldn't see the loopy smile that spread across my face.

"Consider it payback for helping me rescue Kevin."

"Even after the rope incident?"

He chuckled.

"Is the coffee on?" I asked.

"Made it myself."

"I'll pick up the donuts on the way."

"That's a myth, you know," he said.

"What?"

"That police officers spend their mornings hanging out at donut shops, stuffing their faces."

"I got you. I'll make it a dozen of the glazed."

"Good." He hung up.

Slowly I replaced the receiver. Morning coffee with Detective Billie. Now, that's what I deemed a wake-up call.

Kong barked and scratched at the front door. *Okay, first things first.* I threw back the covers and hopped out of bed, a spring to my step.

However, first contact with the cold parquet floor brought me back to reality. I padded to the large window at the front of my Airstream and rubbed at the ice-encrusted glass.

Frost blanketed every leaf of foliage outside. The palm trees looked as though the fronds had been dipped in white chocolate.

"Are you sure you want to go out?" I asked my poodle.

He clawed at the aluminum door again.

"All right." I donned my Windbreaker over my flannel pajamas and slipped into my running shoes. Then I wrapped an old woolen scarf around my head. Fashion conscience, be damned. This was survival.

I fastened the leash to Kong's collar and led him out of the Airstream.

Teeth chattering, I decided against heading for Kong's nemesis—the beach. No need to drag out this painful operation. We sped over to a clump of bougainvillea bushes, where he did his thing.

I took advantage of the time by spying on my neighbors in the behemoth RV. Everything was quiet. Blast it. If I had to be up this early, why shouldn't they?

I scanned their site. Nothing new. Awning still up, picnic table still unused. Except . . . My glance sharpened. A cherry red Ford Escort rental car stood parked to one side. I didn't remember seeing that vehicle before. It seemed kinda low end for a famous couple, but maybe that was part of the whole incognito thing.

Very interesting. If they were exploring the area in a rental with Florida plates, it meant they'd probably be here for a few more days at least. I still had time to find out their identities.

I vowed to keep an eye out for the Ford Escort as I drove around the island.

An hour later, I pulled Rusty into a parking space outside the police station. Checking my appearance in the rearview mirror one more time, I tucked a stray red curl behind my ear and removed the lipstick streaks that had smudged my front teeth.

Okay, so I'd put on a little makeup and washed my curls in Kong's favorite country-apple shampoo. Nothing wrong with sprucing up. Or putting on a pair of neatly pressed jeans and cream colored V-neck sweater. Nothing wrong at all.

I couldn't wear jeans *every* day.

As I let myself into the police station, I noticed that

the receptionist's desk was empty, but, true to his word, Detective Billie had a pot of my favorite caffeinated beverage brewing.

"Hi." He stood in the doorway of his office, looking dark and handsome and dangerous. Dark and handsome for obvious reasons. Dangerous because he made my legs wobble every time I saw him.

"Hi, yourself." I held up the box of donuts.

He grinned. "Grab yourself a cup of coffee, and come on back."

I filled a mug with the steaming black liquid, inhaled the caffeine fumes a few times, and strolled into his office.

"How much longer is this cold spell going to last?" I asked, setting the box on his desk.

He helped himself to a donut. "Don't know. Last year we had almost ten days when the temperature dipped to freezing. People had to scramble to keep their mango groves heated enough to protect the trees."

Detective Billie took a large bite out of his donut. Then he pulled out a manila folder and flipped it open. "Tom's cause of death was drowning."

"So it was an accident?"

"Not necessarily."

My nerves tensed.

"Tom also experienced trauma to the back of the head," he said.

"What does that mean?"

His dark eyes turned opaque. "Someone hit him with a blunt object from behind—probably knocked him unconscious. Then he fell overboard and drowned."

"Do you know what you're saying? The only other person on the boat was Kevin—"

"I'm well aware of that." His mouth tightened. "But I can't hide from the facts or pretend that this is just an accident. Someone deliberately caused Tom to drown, and I have to find out who it was, even if I don't like it. That's my job."

"But Kevin is only a little boy," I protested.

"I'll do everything I can to protect him. The night we picked him up, I went easy on him and asked only a few questions, but I'll have to talk to him again—press for details."

"I know . . . but it stinks."

"Tell me about it." His voice took on a hard edge. "I took this job to keep the community safe, not interrogate kids."

"Actually, I have a theory about Tom's death—"

"Based on your many years of studying criminal justice." The edge became even edgier as he cut in.

"Okay, so I don't have any formal training. But I did help solve that murder case last summer."

"Correct me if I'm wrong, but, as I recall, you were a suspect at first. Then you meddled in my investigation and almost got yourself killed by trying to get the murderer to confess."

"If you start splitting hairs, we're not going to get

anywhere." I set the mug on his desk with undue force. The liquid spilled over the rim and onto the shiny mahogany finish. "Sorry."

He didn't make a move to wipe it up. I dabbed at it with my hand, causing the coffee to drip onto the floor. Not wanting to make it any worse, I halted my mop-up attempts. *Motormouth* and *clumsy.*

"If you didn't want to hear my ideas, why did you ask me to have coffee with you this morning?" Okay, I'd put it out there. The ball was in his court now.

A half smile turned up one side of his mouth. "Maybe I wanted to see if your red hair would heat up my office."

The ball was back in my court now, and I double-faulted. "Has it?"

"Can't say yet."

I briefly retrieved my mug and gulped down another swig of coffee. Forget the balls and the courts. I'd never win at verbal volleys with Detective Billie. One compliment and I turned to mush—or, worse, a motormouth. "Let's say for argument's sake that you've been properly warmed by the sight of my hair. How about letting me give you my hypothesis?"

He leaned back in his chair. "Okay. Shoot."

"Kevin and Tom were alone in the boat when they left the marina, right?"

He nodded.

"They anchored off the mangroves in the late afternoon and fished until evening. After five or six hours of being on the water, Kevin probably fell asleep early.

Not long after Kevin was snoozing, someone could've driven up a second boat, come aboard, and knocked Tom unconscious. Simple, huh?"

"That wouldn't be my word for your theory."

I leaned forward and propped my elbows on his desk. "You don't really think Kevin did it, do you?"

"I don't want to." He sighed. "But he's been an angry boy for the last six months. Mad at his parents, mad at the other kids at school, mad at the world." He stared down at his coffee mug. "A couple weeks ago I had to question him about some vandalism at the island center. Nothing would stick, but I had my suspicions."

I refrained from relating what Kevin's classmate had told me. No need to add fuel to that fire.

Nick cleared his throat. "I'm going over to Sally Jo's house later today to talk to him."

"Do you mind if I'm present?"

"Yes, I mind. I mind like hell." His head jerked up. "I appreciate your help rescuing Kevin, and I gave you the autopsy results as a thank you, but that doesn't mean I'm going to allow you to interfere with my investigation."

"Kevin's well-being concerns me. I don't want to see him hurt or—"

"Neither do I," he cut in swiftly. "Which is why it's best that you leave the police work to me."

"Let me remind you, you're supposed to share information with the press, and I'm the sole investigative reporter for the *Observer*." I was desperate enough to play the journalism card.

"I just did. I told you the cause of Tom's death."

Damn. He trumped me. Winning games—mental or physical—was not my forte.

"I'm also Wanda Sue's friend. I can't just turn a blind eye when her grandson might be accused of murder."

"It's not a 'blind eye' when you let the police do their job." He leaned toward me. "A young boy's future is at stake, and I can't let anyone jeopardize the investigation. It could end up hurting Kevin even more."

"So you've already made up your mind that he's the culprit—"

"I didn't say that."

"Not in so many words."

He help up his hands. "Why is it we always end up arguing? Especially when, in this instance, we both want what's best for Kevin?"

"I don't know. Maybe because we each like doing things our own way." I sighed. "Still . . . I thought we were becoming . . . friends."

"Is that what you think we are?"

"Maybe." I straightened, letting my arms stretch across his desk.

"I don't feel like kissing my *friends* when they disagree with me." His fingers touched mine.

Whoa! Electric shocks fired through my body all the way to my toes. I snatched my hand back. Little good it did me. I could still feel the charge in every nerve ending.

A dark flush spread across his face, and his features

shuttered. "But don't think that means I have any intention of behaving in an unprofessional way. I have my
job to do. People on this island depend on me, and I'm
not about to betray that trust."

The electric aftershocks fizzled out.

"Kevin's family has already experienced one loss,
and I don't want to add to their heartache," he continued.

"Me, either. That's why I shared my theory with you."
Suddenly I didn't know where to look. I didn't want him
to see the disappointment in my eyes.

"Duly noted."

*Oh, great. Now he's back to Mr. Reserved, by-the-
book cop.* "Is this about Kevin or the other case—the
one on the reservation?" I inquired gently.

His hands balled into fists. "That case has been over
for years, I can't go back and fix it."

"What happened?"

"Why should you care?"

"Call me a glutton for punishment, but I'd like to
know."

A tiny muscle began working in his jaw. I'd known
Nick Billie long enough to realize, when he clenched his
jaw like that, something big was going on inside him.

"There isn't much to tell. I was working as a tribal
police officer on the Miccosukee Reservation. I'd been
there a couple of years, covering routine crimes. Petty
theft. Disorderly behavior. Occasional domestic distur-
bances. Pretty run-of-the-mill stuff. I thought I was
the king of the walk, keeping the reservation free of the

type of crime that was everywhere in southern Florida. Then a boy went missing. The parents seemed really torn up about it, doing everything they could to help me find him." He drew in a deep breath and exhaled. "To make a long story short, turns out the father had his son doing drug runs through the Everglades. A dealer got mad and shot the boy. When his body finally appeared, the father confessed to everything."

I shuddered. "How awful."

"Yeah. Turns out a drug ring was operating right under my nose, and I was too conceited to see it. Even worse, I never did find the drug dealer who killed the boy." He shook his head in regret. "I couldn't stay there after that. I took a job with the Naples police department for a couple of years, then I came here."

"You can't blame yourself for that boy's death. How could you have known—"

"It's my *job* to know what's going on." A fist came down on the desk—hard. "If I'd been paying more attention to the subtle clues around me, I would've found out about the drug ring. I was stupid, and I made mistakes that cost a young boy his life."

"Seems like his father was the one to blame."

"He got a jail sentence—eight years. Can you believe that?"

"He should've gotten life. I still think you're taking responsibility for events that were out of your control."

"I'll be the judge of that."

I was suddenly torn by conflicting desires. On the

one hand, I wanted to put my arms around him in comfort, but on the other I wanted to shake some sense into him. Not knowing which would be best, I did neither.

He flipped the manila folder shut and, with it, the door to his past. "I'll issue press releases at appropriate times as the case develops."

I stood up. His words clearly signaled dismissal. "I can't promise you that I won't try to find out who killed Tom Crawford."

"And I can't promise you that I won't lock you up if you get in my way."

"Friends?"

He smiled. "Of course."

I set the empty coffee mug on his desk and left.

Chapter Nine

I drove the short distance to the *Observer* office, weighing the whole structure of events that had just occurred. I now knew two things.

Tom Crawford's death was no accident. And if I was going to help Wanda Sue, I had to find out who came aboard that boat and knocked Tom into the water. Whatever tiny doubts I had that Kevin did it, I squashed immediately. That terrified little boy I'd comforted in the boat cabin couldn't have hurt his father.

I also had learned why Detective Billie took his job so seriously: He didn't want to repeat mistakes from his past. Just knowing that made him seem more human, more vulnerable, and more compellingly attractive.

And don't forget he said he'd like to kiss you.

I started, causing my foot to ram down the gas pedal.

It stuck, of course, and I almost plowed into a Volvo station wagon with a DOG ON BOARD sign. I jammed on the brakes, and, luckily, they worked. Still, I narrowly missed rear-ending the vehicle with its slobbering black Labrador hanging out the passenger window.

I took in a long, calming breath.

Don't forget: Nick also immediately regretted saying it. He'd shut down when he realized what he said, just as I'd pulled back when he touched my hand. I sighed. Maybe neither of us wanted that kind of pulse-pounding, heart-stopping, breathless, in-your-face relationship. It was too messy. Too tempting. Too life-shattering.

Right now keeping my life on track was taking up all my energy. One wrong move and I'd lose my job. I'd be Mixed-up Mallie again, roaming the highways, looking for the bluebird of happiness—and never finding it.

Get a grip. Keep your focus. That had to be my mantra.

I parked Rusty and strolled into the office. But I stopped in my tracks when I came face-to-face with the beady black eyes of Madame Geri's bird, Marley.

"Mallie, look who showed up." Sandy pointed, quite unnecessarily, at the island psychic. As if I could overlook a woman with gray deadlocks wearing a fifties poodle skirt and cardigan and sporting a parrot on her shoulder.

I leveled an accusatory glance at Sandy, who spread her palms in an it-wasn't-me gesture.

"*I* called Mom," Jimmy piped up. "I thought you might be able to use her spiritual guidance." He and Sandy were seated at her desk, paging through our latest edition of the *Observer.*

"I don't need that kind of help to—"

"You want to find out who killed Tom Crawford?" Madame Geri asked.

"How do you know he was murdered?"

"Was he murdered?" Jimmy and Sandy blurted simultaneously, heads swiveling toward me.

"Can't really say." I fastened my glance on Madame Geri. "Where do you get your info?"

She looked affronted. "The spirit world tells me what I want to know."

"If he *was* murdered, I don't suppose the spirits told you who did it," I inquired, trying not to let sarcasm creep into my voice.

"Doesn't work that way. Some things in life have to be figured out on their own. Then people learn the lessons they're supposed to."

Somehow I'd known she'd say something like that.

"You can't mess with fate," Jimmy added.

"Bad karma." Sandy nodded sagely. "Madame Geri can help and protect you, Mallie."

I blinked a couple of times, hoping that I was merely hallucinating from an overindulgence of donuts and caffeine. No such luck. Madame Geri was still parked next to my desk, her bird giving me the evil eye.

"Does Anita know about this?" I asked in desperation. When in doubt, evoke Anita's name—it was always guaranteed to dampen any group's optimism.

"She sure does."

I didn't need to turn around. I knew that gravelly voice only too well. She motioned at me with her bony fingers.

Silently I trudged into my boss' office.

Once Anita shut the door, I turned to her. "You've got to be kidding. You actually want me to haul around that pseudo-psychic?"

"Sure do." She seated herself at her desk and folded her arms.

"Why?"

"Look, kiddo. I don't believe she's psychic any more than the man in moon, but people talk to her. They tell her things they wouldn't tell their own mothers. And somewhere in all that touchy-feely garbage could be a gem of truth—maybe even the reason Tom Crawford was killed."

"How did you find out he was murdered?"

"I never reveal a source." She smiled. I swallowed hard. In spite of her trying to cut out the cigarettes, after twenty years of chain smoking, her teeth weren't a pretty sight.

"Take Madame Geri with you for a couple of days. See if she can dig up any gossip. If nothing turns up, dump her. And don't forget, I gotta have the initial story about Kevin's rescue and his father's possible homicide by the end of the day. Keep your eye on the ball, kiddo." Anita waved me out of her office. Sentimental, she wasn't.

I exited, closing the door with a distinct thud to let her know I wasn't happy with the prospect of babysitting a New Age quack. I heard a short bark of laughter in response. I gritted my teeth. There was no use fighting it; once Anita made up her mind, I had to do it.

"Looks like it's you and me, Madame Geri." I moved toward my desk.

"And Marley." She stroked the turquoise feathers of her beady-eyed bird.

"No way. No birds in my truck." I dug around in my drawer until I found an unused notepad.

Marley squawked, and I jumped back, dropping the pad. "Well . . . maybe he can ride along, but don't let him do anything weird."

She pursed her mouth. "My bird is well trained. He does only what I tell him to do."

"Oh." I made a mental note not to anger Madame Geri. I didn't want Marley pecking out my eyes before lunchtime.

"I want to see Tom's boat." Madame Geri stood up, clutching her leather bag to her chest. Then she tottered toward the door, with Marley firmly fixed on his perch, and I wondered if his claws were digging into her shoulders. *Ouch.*

"Let's get a move on. Time's a wastin'." Madame Geri used her hip to nudge open the door.

I leveled my own version of a beady-eyed glance in Sandy's direction. She gave a sheepish shrug. Surrendering to the inevitable, I vowed to take revenge on

Sandy later by cutting off the price tags from the next outfit she wore into the office.

I led Madame Geri to my truck, keeping a healthy distance between Marley and me.

"Nice set of wheels," she commented as she climbed into the passenger seat. Marley tucked his head under a wing and shifted to the other shoulder so she could fasten the seat belt.

Oh, goody. Now he was on my side. He'd have quick access if he wanted to peck out my eyes.

I slid into the driver's seat, leaning as far to the left as I could without actually hanging out the window. I cranked up the engine and backed out of the parking lot, aware of every feather movement.

"Look, Madame Geri, I think you and I should put our cards on the table—and I don't mean Tarot." I pressed down the gas pedal, causing Rusty to peak at his top speed of 50mph and, with it, my motormouth kicked into gear. "I don't believe in psychics. I worked for a so-called psychic hotline for a while, and I know what goes on there. The whole purpose of my job was to keep people talking so they'd rack up a lot of minutes. The longer they were on the phone, the more money the company made. I never met a single person at the hotline who could predict the future—including me. The only thing we knew for sure was that we'd be fired if we didn't make a certain quota every day. I'm not proud of what I did. All I can say is, I was between jobs and needed the money. . . ." *The story of my life.*

"Did you hurt anybody?"

"I guess not."

"Then what was the harm?"

I thought for a few seconds. "I pretended to be something I wasn't. Tried to convince people to confide in me so I could make money off them."

"Bah." She shrugged. "They knew you weren't a psychic. They wanted an ear to listen to them. And you fit the bill. Everyone ended up with what they wanted."

"You sound more like a pragmatist than a psychic."

"Same thing. I see the world as it is, not the way people want it to be. That's psychic *and* practical."

"So you don't just tell people what they want to hear?" *Hah. Answer that with a straight face.*

She shook her head. "The spirit world would never let me. And it doesn't pay to anger the spirits."

"What would they do? Flip on your TV in the middle of the night?"

Her fingers tapped my arm, and she nodded knowingly. " 'There's more in heaven and earth than you've ever dreamed of' . . . Shakespeare. Your favorite poet."

"Good guess." *How in the world did she know that?* "Sandy must've told you I was a comparative literature major in a previous life."

"No. She didn't." Madame Geri closed her eyes and leaned back against the tattered headrest. "Believing in something greater than yourself scares you, but your fears make you foolish. Your task in this life is to deepen your spirituality . . . connect on the soul level. But you'll only do it if you stop—"

"And smell the roses?" I cut in, refusing to hear any more of her half-baked predictions. They were nutty, off-the-wall and, all of a sudden, way too close to the truth. "I'm not interested in your psychobabble."

"Suit yourself." Her eyelids rose once more. "But if you want a Tarot reading sometime, I'll fill you in on what you need to know."

"Thanks—I may take you up on that offer sometime." *When hell freezes over.*

Speaking of freezing . . . I cranked up Rusty's heater. We rode the rest of the way in silence punctuated only by periodic squawks from Marley when he spotted other birds outside the truck. The sounds reverberated through Rusty's small cab, and I was ready to toss him and Madame Geri out the door by the time we reached the Trade Winds Marina.

"Here we are." I parked by the docks. Marley emitted another eardrum-piercing squawk when he spied the pelicans, and I jumped out of Rusty before he had a chance to damage my hearing any further.

"Hey, Mallie!" someone shouted.

I turned toward the office and saw Pete Cresswell striding toward me.

"Have you recovered from your boat trip?" he asked as he grinned and engulfed me in a bear hug.

"Almost."

"What's up?"

"You not going to believe this, but I got stuck with the island psychic as a sidekick." I scanned the docks. "Where's Tom's boat? I need to look at it."

"I guess it would be okay. Nick Billie already had it checked out early this morning as a crime scene and removed the yellow tape." He frowned. "Sad to think somebody killed Tom."

At that point, Madame Geri made an appearance, sans Marley, her heels tapping a staccato beat on the wooden docks.

"Madame Geri," Pete said, a note of awe touching his voice, as if he'd acknowledged royalty. "It's an honor."

"Not you too?" I murmured under my breath.

"We need to see the boat, please." Madame Geri spoke in a regal tone.

Pete offered his arm and escorted her down the docks.

I trailed behind them, mumbling to myself.

When we reached the small, run-down fishing boat, Madame Geri released Pete's arm and paced back and forth in front of the vessel. *What is* that *supposed to do?*

"How in the world were you able to persuade Madame Geri to work with you?" Pete asked.

I grimaced. "Made her an offer she couldn't refuse?"

Pete flashed a warning glance in my direction. "Madame Geri knows her stuff. If anyone can find out what happened to Tom, she can."

"Oh, *please,*" I moaned. "What hold does this woman have over the island?"

"We respect her. She's a true psychic."

"So everybody keeps telling me." I watched as Madame Geri reached into her leather bag and pulled out a crystal on a string. "Got any ideas on who might've killed Tom?"

"I can't say for sure . . . all I've heard is gossip. But some of the guys around the docks said Sally Jo was seeing somebody on the side."

"You know who?"

"Nope. But you might stop by the Seafood Shanty and talk to Nora. She might know."

"Okay. We'll head over there for lunch after we wrap it up here." I pulled out my Official Reporter's Note-pad. "What about Jake Fowler? I heard he hated Tom because their clam farm went belly up."

Pete nodded. "Jake sure was sore about that . . . but I don't know if he was mad enough to kill Tom."

"When I met Jake at the elementary school with his son, he seemed to have quite a temper."

"Guess so. But Tom was no angel, either—especially when he'd had too many beers."

"According to Wanda Sue, he was on the wagon," I informed him. "You know where I can find Jake?"

Pete looked over his left shoulder at the large boats docked near the marina office. "His shrimp boat is in. . . . He might be at the Seafood Shanty for lunch. A lot of the fishermen hang out there. Again—check with Nora."

"Gotcha." I jotted down a few notes and tossed the pad into my canvas bag.

Madame Geri began chanting and waving the crystal.

"May I go aboard?" I asked.

"Sure." Pete helped me onto the boat. Once there, I strolled toward the open deck in the back. The bow? Stern? I forgot. Whatever it was called, I nosed around it. Surprisingly, for such an aging vessel, it was clean and orderly. The fishing nets rested neatly stacked on one side. Two pairs of "island Reeboks" were aligned behind the captain's chair. Tackle boxes were open, but lures and hooks had been placed with care in their appropriate sections. One thing was certain—Tom kept a tidy boat.

I peered into the small cabin. Nothing much there, either. Just a few Styrofoam cups on the counter and a coffeepot, still holding remnants of a previously made brew.

Nothing out of the ordinary to suggest that a struggle had taken place on the boat.

All at once Madame Geri let out a loud scream.

What now?

Chapter Ten

I dashed to the back of the boat and beheld Madame Geri, standing on the dock with her eyes closed and features contorted in pain, yelling at the top of her lungs.

"What's happening? Are you all right?" I hopped off the boat and raced to where she stood.

"I see water . . . death!" she wailed.

So tell me something I don't know. "Please. Quiet down. They're going to call the police if you keep this up."

Actually, the fishermen at their nets had offered a flicker of interest, then returned to their work.

They obviously knew Madame Geri.

She lowered her volume to a soft moan.

"What did you see?" I asked.

"Water . . . panic . . . loss. His entire life passed

through his mind the last few moments. He didn't want to lose his son, his wife. It was all gone. All over . . ." She shuddered and moaned, her head swaying back and forth.

"Can you take it back a little further in time? How did he end up in the water?"

Madame Geri peeped open one eye. "Don't rush the spirits. They'll give me information when they're good and ready." The eye snapped shut again.

I gritted my teeth and waited.

She dropped her chin to her chest and chanted a few unintelligible words. "A sharp pain. Yes, a pain in the back of the head. It hurt so much. The world exploded in a shower of colors. . . ." She winced as though in pain. "Why?"

"That's the million-dollar question," I murmured under my breath. Okay, so Madame Geri's contacts were disembodied spirits, but did they have to be so obtuse? "Could you ask them who hit Tom on the head?"

"Nope." She shook herself and opened her eyes. "That's all for today."

"The spirit world seems a bit capricious," I said.

"They live in a different dimension, governed by different rules. We can't pretend to understand their intent."

"If you say so." And with Madame Geri as their sole contact with the human world, I probably had very little chance of learning *anything* that would help me solve Tom's murder. "I checked out the boat but didn't find—"

She clucked her tongue and brushed past me. Craning her neck over the side of the boat, she scanned the deck. "What's that?"

I followed her pointed finger. Wedged in a corner, half covered by an ice chest, was a brightly colored fishing fly. I jumped back onto the boat and retrieved it. "It's odd . . . sort of a fishlike shape attached to a hook."

Madame Geri studied it. "It's a deceiver."

"A what?"

"A deceiver. Tubing along the shank with side wings. Yup, it's a deceiver, all right."

"I take it a deceiver is a kind of fishing fly," I said with some asperity.

She nodded. "A very special kind of fly. It's made to appear like live bait to fool larger fish."

"Oh, I get it now. It 'deceives' the fish into thinking it's alive." I turned it over in my palm. "Is it handmade? I mean, could Tom have made it?"

"Not unless he was a skilled fly maker. This particular one took a lot of time and effort—it's handcrafted with real feathers. Most of the men on this island make flies, but just your basic designs."

Cautious, I narrowed my eyes. "How do you know all this?"

"My father was a fisherman."

"Oh." *Who'd've thunk it?* "So someone might've given him this fly . . . someone who knew how to make such an elaborate one?"

"That would be my guess."

I stroked the white and chartreuse feathers, careful to avoid the hook. "Who would know how to make a lure like this?"

She shrugged. "Someone who's spent a lifetime learning the craft. A master fly builder."

"Can you contact the spirit world for a name and telephone number?"

Madame Geri's eyes narrowed. "It isn't good karma to joke about the next world."

"I don't take this world seriously, so why should I take the next one as anything more than a joke?"

She smiled. "Life has a lot of lessons for you. Not all of them are going to be to your liking." Without another word, she tottered toward Rusty.

I was left with the deceiver in my palm and not a snappy comeback in sight. Wouldn't you know?

Half an hour later, we pulled up to the Seafood Shanty. I needed food, and I wanted to follow up on Pete's tip that I talk to his wife, Nora. If Sally Jo had been having an affair, Nora would know. As a waitress at the Shanty, she had a pipeline to every dirty little secret on Coral Island and then some. And I wanted to question Jake Fowler if he were there.

I accepted the futility of trying to dump Madame Geri and simply escorted her inside. Marley remained in the truck again, thank goodness.

"Hey, Mallie, how's it going?" Nora waved me over to a small table in the back of the large dining room.

The Seafood Shanty boasted a nautical décor, complete with fishing nets draped across the ceiling and anchors hanging on the wall behind the bar. The owners had tried to attract a higher class of tourist clientele by painting FAMILY RESTAURANT on the outside, but the place was still largely home to fishermen and bikers.

Today it was almost deserted, except for a few fishermen huddled around a table in the back of the room. *Bingo.* I spied Jake Fowler's crew cut and harsh features.

Nora hugged me. She looked great. Her previously brassy blond hair had grown out to its normal shade of chestnut, and her skin glowed. When I pulled back, her gaze moved toward my companion. Her eyes widened. "Madame Geri, so nice to see you."

My psychic companion inclined her head.

Nora pulled out a chair for Madame Geri, and she settled into it, folding her hands with almost regal composure. She was a queen all right—a monarch of mystic mumbo jumbo.

"What can I get for you?" Nora handed us menus.

We each ordered one of the few edible items: a cheeseburger with fries. I didn't even have time to request coffee before Nora grabbed the menus, saying, "I'll put on a new pot for you."

I smiled in gratitude.

Nora reappeared in no time with our drinks. As she set a steaming cup of java in front of me, my mood improved tenfold.

"Here's your coffee, Madame Geri. I brought some fresh milk and two packets of sugar. I know how you like yours extra sweet." Nora acted as if she were serving a celebrity. *Jeez.*

"That's just fine. Thanks." Madame Geri stirred in the milk and sugar, then took a sip and scanned Nora. "When are you due?"

Nora's mouth dropped open. "How did you know? We haven't told anyone—"

Madame Geri smiled.

"Due? What do you mean?" I looked from one to the other. "Are you—"

"Pregnant." Nora nodded with a soft curve to her lips. "Just found out two days ago. I'm due in July."

Madame Geri touched Nora's stomach. "You want to know if it's a boy or girl?"

"Nope. We want to be surprised."

"I don't blame you." She removed her hand. "The baby's healthy . . . that's the important thing."

"It sure is."

I listened with bewilderment. What the heck was going on?

"Being on your feet all day might be a strain during the pregnancy," Madame Geri pointed out.

"That's what Pete and I thought. I got my GED. a few weeks ago, so I'm going to work in the marina office as a bookkeeper. I always was good with figures."

"That's great, Nora." I finally found my voice.

She beamed. "I'll be back with your order in two shakes." As she moved away, I noticed a perky lilt to her step.

"Okay—dish." I placed my palms on the table. "Who told you about the pregnancy?"

"The baby, of course."

"The baby?" I laughed.

"He spoke to me the minute we arrived. Told me how happy he will be to have parents like Nora and Pete. I think he's very lucky." She placed a finger to her lips. "Don't breathe a word that I let slip it's a boy."

My chin dropped to my chest. "I give up. You should win an Academy Award," I mumbled, half to myself.

We drank our coffee in silence.

In a short time Nora served our lunches. My mouth watered at the sight of my charbroiled cheeseburger. The Seafood Shanty was a tad on the dingy side, but their burgers were second to none. Madame Geri gave a gracious nod for her similar repast.

"Nora, can you spare us a few minutes?" I settled the paper towel, which passed for a napkin, on my lap.

"Sure, honey." She set her tray on a nearby empty table. "We're hardly going gangbusters today." She seated herself between Madame Geri and me.

I took a bite of my cheeseburger and swallowed in delight. "You probably heard about Tom Crawford."

Nora's face stilled and grew serious. "Yeah. What a cryin' shame."

"I talked with Detective Billie this morning and . . . well, do you know anyone who might have had a grudge against Tom?" I poured ketchup over my fries.

Nora's mouth tightened. "Frank King."

"Who's he?" I immediately pulled my notepad out of my canvas bag.

"A no-good, wife-stealing jerk." Nora's mouth drew into a tight line.

I dug out my pen, downing a few fries on the way. "Could you be more specific?"

"He's a local fisherman who started hitting on Sally Jo the moment she and Tom separated. I swear, that man was like a shark circling its prey . . . just waiting for the right moment to make his move. And with Sally Jo being so vulnerable . . ." She waved a hand in disgust.

"Were they having an affair?"

"Can't say for sure, but if I had to give an opinion, it would be yes."

"You think Frank was in love with Sally Jo?" I picked up my cheeseburger and took a few more bites.

"Dunno. But he sure was taken with her. Always has been. They were high school sweethearts, but she broke up with him when she started going out with Tom."

I paused midbite, remembering Sam's words: "Lust might be motivation for murder."

Nora turned to Madame Geri, who'd been quietly consuming her lunch, and asked, "What do you think?"

"Unclear. The spirits haven't passed anything on to

me yet." She glanced at me. "I'll let you know when they do."

"Thanks. I, for one, will be waiting with bated breath," I said dryly, then turned to Nora. "Where can I find Frank? I'd like to talk to him."

"He runs the Fish and Bait Shoppe next to the Trade Winds Marina. He's usually there every day."

"Thanks." I reached into my canvas bag and pulled out the fishing fly. "Hey, since Pete is a fisherman, could you tell me on the QT if you've seen something like this before?"

"Nice deceiver." She let out a low whistle of appreciation. "Looks handmade and first rate."

"You know who could've made it?"

"Lots of guys on the island make flies." She touched the feathers. "But only one person I know has the skill to make a deceiver like this—Frank King."

"You don't say." I wrapped the fishing fly in a napkin and placed it back in my canvas bag. "Do you think Tom would've let Frank come aboard his boat under any circumstances?" I offered Nora some French fries, hoping she wouldn't ask me to reveal any details about Tom's death.

"Sure. They were friends . . . worked on the shrimp boats together." Nora helped herself to a couple of fries.

"What about Jake Fowler? Would Tom have let him aboard?"

"Jake?" Her eyebrows arched. "No way. They hated each other."

"And I take it Tom didn't know that Frank might've been seeing Sally Jo on the side."

"You got it." She nodded with a knowing smile. "Tom was totally in the dark about that. But you know men—they're clueless."

"Tell me about it." I rolled my eyes.

"Like a certain tall, dark, and handsome detective?" Nora's eyes sparkled with deliberate intent. "What do you think, Madame Geri? Would Mallie and Nick Billie make a good couple? Let's see. Mallie Billie? Nah."

"Nora . . ." I warned. The last thing I needed was the island's freelance psychic assessing my love life—or lack thereof. "How 'bout the check?" I reached into my canvas bag for my wallet.

"It's on the house."

"What?"

"My boss would never let Madame Geri pay for her own lunch. Her predictions saved him a ton of money last year when she told him to have the plumbing checked at his house. Turns out all the pipes were corroded and ready to burst. He would've had a lot of water damage if he hadn't listened to her." Nora moved off toward the kitchen.

I glanced at Madame Geri. She nodded, a self-satisfied expression on her face. This was her territory, and she knew it. Everybody trusted her. I was still the outsider, looked upon with suspicion and caution.

Drat her anyway. "I'll be right back." I grabbed my Official Reporter's Notepad and strolled toward the table in the back. Two grizzled fishermen eyed me; one tapped Jake on the shoulder and gestured in my direction. Jake leveled a scowl at me.

I cleared my throat. "Mr. Fowler, could I speak to you for a few minutes? We met at the elementary sch—"

"I remember," he interrupted. His dark eyes raked over me. "Whaddya want?"

"You've heard about Tom Crawford's death?" I assumed my "reporter's voice"—learned by imitating television news anchors.

He gave a quick jerk of his head.

"Do you have any comments for the *Observer*? I heard that the two of you were once business partners."

His hands balled into fists. "I got nothing to say."

I swallowed hard, trying to remember my Tae Kwon Do training in case those large fists came in my direction. "Were you still angry with him about your bankruptcy?"

"Who told you that?" he demanded.

"Just heard it around."

His features kindled in anger. "I didn't hurt him, if that's what you're getting at."

I met his glance squarely. "I never said that."

Jake lurched to his feet. "I'm not telling you nothing else."

I tensed, my breath catching in my throat. He topped me by a good six inches and had a beefy build. But I stood my ground, in spite of my shaking knees. "I'd be happy to talk to you later—"

"Get outta of my way," he grated out as he pushed past me, knocking over a chair.

The other men at the table trooped out silently.

I exhaled, and the tension slowly drained out of my body, causing my knees to shake in reaction. Somehow I managed to stumble back to my table, where Madame Geri and Marley waited.

"That went rather well, don't you think?" I said.

"Like a lead balloon," she quipped.

I didn't dare sit down because I wasn't sure I could get back up again. "Let's hit the road."

I drove back to the *Observer* office, turned Madame Geri and Marley over to her son, and dashed off my story about Kevin's rescue and his dad's suspicious death. Reading it over once, I placed a hard copy on Anita's desk. True to form, she immediately attacked it with her red pen.

So it wasn't great. I'd made the deadline.

As reaction from the day's events set in, I suddenly felt worn out, weary. I needed the comfort of my Airstream and time to gather my scattered wits. Waving good-bye to Sandy, I headed for the Twin Palms at Mango Bay.

As I approached my site, I noticed the Wanderlodge still parked next to me in all its glory. But the rental car was gone, so I assumed the mystery RV'ers were exploring the island.

Aha. My big chance to snoop around. I hopped out of my truck and tiptoed toward the front of the gigantic

RV. Curtains were drawn around the front windows, but I tried to peer inside anyway. I couldn't make out anything. Moving around to the side, I checked the windows under the awning. One shade was pulled up slightly.

Rubbing my hands with glee, I craned my neck to bring my eyes level with the open area. *Wow.* The interior was incredible. A white leather sectional sofa, plush white carpet throughout, and real wood cabinets with lights overhead.

Whoever lived in this mammoth vehicle had money coming out the wazoo.

"Is there a problem, Mallie?"

I whirled around. It was Pop Pop Welch, the Twin Palms' wizened maintenance man. "Uh, no. Well . . . I'm not sure. I thought I . . . uh . . . smelled gas or something."

"A leak in the line?" He drew closer and sniffed.

"Possibly." I swallowed hard. It sounded lame, even to me.

"I'll call Wanda Sue and have it checked out." His wrinkled hands reached for the two-way radio on his belt.

I hightailed it over to my Airstream and let myself in before Pop Pop could ask for further details about the fabricated gas leak. Kong barked his usual enthusiastic greeting, and I scooped him up into my arms. As he licked my face something silly, I cranked up the heat and sat down to think.

Chapter Eleven

Two hours later, I'd completed a quick recap of murder suspects.

Jake Fowler. He certainly seemed to have the motive and capability to murder Tom. I made a mental note to find out if he had an alibi for the night Tom was killed.

Frank King. If he were having an affair with Sally Jo, it was possible he wanted Tom out of the way—permanently.

I wrote down Sally Jo's name next to his. A dissatisfied and estranged wife, she could've been in on Frank's plot to get rid of her husband.

Could one of them be "Salty Surfer," who'd sent me the threatening, albeit poorly written, e-mail? Unfortunately, there was a block on the IP address, and I couldn't trace it back to the writer. Salty but smart.

I paused, then slowly wrote another name. *Kevin.* I found it hard to believe that he could've killed his own father, but . . . I couldn't let myself go there.

First chance, I needed to talk to Kevin. It was very possible that he'd heard something on the boat that would provide clues to the murderer's identity. Then I needed to fill in Nick Billie on everything that had happened.

Right now, I had only one clue: the fancy handmade fly that Madame Geri found on the boat.

I retrieved the deceiver from my canvas bag and examined it more carefully. Beautiful chartreuse and white feathers fanned out from the tiny, fish-shaped form attached to the hook, the eyes black, the scales blue and silver. Obviously it had been crafted with loving care. Whoever had fashioned this fly had combined the love of fishing with art.

A deceiver. Had someone left it behind in haste? Was it the kind of object "Salty Surfer" would make?

I brushed my fingers along the feathers. They felt real. A fishing fly made with *real* feathers? Now that probably *was* distinctive.

Kong jumped down and scampered toward the front door. He looked at me with expectant eyes.

"All right. But we're heading toward the beach. I need some sea air."

He slumped into a sitting position and covered his eyes with his front paws.

After slipping into my Windbreaker, I grabbed his

leash and fastened it around his collar. We emerged from the warmth of the Airstream into the damp cold. I hunched my shoulders and flipped up the hood of my jacket.

"Brrrr." A chilly breeze came in off the Gulf, and the sky had turned charcoal gray, readying us for another night of freezing temperatures. *Jeez, I need to move to Florida. Oh, wait. I am in Florida.* It just felt as cold as winter in the Midwest.

Not surprisingly, it took less than two minutes to clear my head. As Kong and I hurried back to the Airstream, I saw Wanda Sue knocking on my door.

Kong barked excitedly at the sight of my landlady.

She turned around and waved. Wearing a red leather coat over green velour pants, she looked like a walking traffic signal. Stop or go, Wanda Sue liked her bright colors.

"Mallie, I wanted to ask you a favor," she began.

"Come in where it's warm." I opened the door and motioned for her to follow me.

Once inside, she settled on my old plaid sofa. Kong parked himself next to her feet and occupied himself with nibbling on the hem of her pants.

"Kong, stop that." I snapped my fingers.

"It's all right. These old pants are ready for a charity bin as it is." She stroked Kong's ears. He growled in response.

"How are you doing?" I asked.

"Okay, I guess. It's Sally Jo who's having the hard

time of it." She smoothed a stray hair behind her ear with a shaky hand. "Would you mind going on over to her place again for a little while? Just for some moral support? I need to stay here 'cause Pop Pop said someone reported a gas leak. We gotta check every site, just to play it safe, and that could take a couple of hours."

"Oh?" I averted my head.

"It's all them dimwit snowbirds. They always think they're smelling gas leaks. They're like chickens with their heads cut off when it comes to propane."

"Yeah, they can be real alarmists." I swung my attention back to Wanda Sue with a guilty grimace. "I'd be happy to go over to Sally Jo's." It was the least I could do after tying up Wanda Sue's geriatric handyman, I added to myself.

"Thank you so much, Mallie." A ghost of a smile spread across her heavily made-up face. "You've been such a good friend to me and Sally Jo through all of this. I don't know what I can do to repay you."

"I'm paying *you* back for giving me a chance to get on my feet when I first moved here. I haven't forgotten how you let me stay a month rent free till I got my first paycheck."

"That was nothing, honey. You've been a sweet pea in a pod."

"Thanks." I couldn't help an inward smile. No matter what, Wanda Sue kept up the steady stream of country clichés.

"I . . . I . . ." Wanda Sue began crying. Kong gazed

up at her and whimpered. After sharing many years of my flaky life, he's always been particularly sensitive to tearful women. I grabbed Kong and hugged Wanda Sue. While both of them bawled in my arms, I prayed that Pop Pop had one of his notorious memory black-outs and would forget that *I* was the dimwit who'd reported the gas leak. All because I couldn't resist nosing around my neighbors' RV.

All thoughts of Pop Pop, the gas leak, and my mysterious neighbors dissolved as I tried to console my landlady and pooch.

Darkness had fallen by the time I pulled up in front of Sally Jo's trailer. It had taken me almost an hour to calm Wanda Sue and Kong down enough so that I could leave them. Eventually Pop Pop picked up Wanda Sue in his golf cart. Luckily, he'd appeared to have forgotten my part in the gas leak incident, and we all joined in on blaming the dimwit tourists.

Wearing a T-shirt, two sweaters, and the Windbreaker, I was fortified against the cold as I headed for Sally Jo's front door. After ringing the bell, I hopped from one foot to the other to keep the circulation going in my legs.

"Why, Mallie, what a nice surprise," Sally Jo drawled as she swung open the door. "Come on in, honey."

I didn't need another invitation.

"This cold snap could freeze the tail off a Florida bobcat." With a shiver, she closed the door.

I guessed losing a tail was similar to humans' freezing

their buns off, but I wasn't quite sure. As I unzipped my Windbreaker, I noticed that Sally Jo looked much better today. Her eyes were still red-rimmed, but the dull, flat expression had cleared. She'd donned a pair of jeans with a white leather fringed top and even wore a little makeup and lipstick. *Much better.* In fact, she looked incredibly good for having just lost her husband two days earlier.

A man cleared his throat.

I swung my head in the direction of the pink sectional sofa. Sitting on one end was a guy possibly in his late twenties. Nice looking in a bland sort of way— brown hair, brown eyes, and a deeply tanned face.

"Uh . . . this is Frank King. He stopped by to pay his respects." Sally Jo's hands fluttered around her face as if she didn't know quite what to do with them. "He's an old friend."

"Hi, I'm Mallie Monroe."

He rose from the sofa and moved toward me. As he smiled and stretched out his hand, I saw a cautious look flash in his eyes. A brief surge . . . then it was gone. But I'd seen it.

Was he the reason for Sally Jo's transformation? The makeup and leather fringe weren't for my visit, that's for sure.

"Sally Jo and I are old high school buddies," he said in a low voice. Suddenly I saw what Sally Jo might find attractive. First of all, he was tall and lean, without an ounce of fat. But besides the hunky build, he had a way of fastening his attention on you as if you were the most special, the most important thing the world. That was a potent attraction for any woman.

"How nice that you could come over in her time of need," I murmured. It sounded like a line from a funeral home commercial, but it was the best I could do. My mind was racing ahead with a dozen unanswered questions.

The phone rang in the kitchen.

"Let me get that. You two just set a spell. . . ." Sally Jo looked as if she wanted to say something else, but the phone's insistent ringing flustered her. "I'll be right back."

Frank and I passed a few awkward, silent moments, then we both started talking at once.

"When did you hear—" I began.

"I've read your articles—" he began.

We both stopped abruptly.

"You go first," he said.

"Thanks." I slipped off my jacket. "So when did you hear about Tom's death?"

He dropped down onto the sofa. "Yesterday. The whole island is talking about it. Poor guy. Rumor has it he took Kevin fishing and fell overboard after too many beers." His voice rose at the end in the form of a question. *He's* fishing, I realized.

So he hadn't received the latest update from the gossip grapevine. "That's the rumor."

"Everybody will sure miss him."

I sat down a little distance away from him. "Were you good friends?"

"Sort of." He hesitated. "We worked together on the shrimp boats for about six years. You get to know a man when you spend weeks at a time cooped up on a small shrimper." He rubbed his hands up and down his jeans-clad thighs, fingers tapping the denim. A nervous reaction?

"What kind of man was he?" I probed.

"Okay when he was sober. But he liked his beer. And when he drank, he could get butt-ugly. You know what I mean? He'd say stuff that could cut you in two. I didn't like that side of him. It made me want to—" He broke off, that cautious look in his eyes again.

"Kill him?"

"No." Frank's whole face tightened as if my words had closed around his head like a vise. "Knock some sense into him."

I watched as he shifted around on the sofa. Even more nervous.

"Of course, I'd never hurt him," Frank continued. "But I sure didn't like the way I saw him treating Sally Jo and Kevin after one of his binges." His tone turned to disgust. "He also had women on the side."

I stiffened. "You mean affairs?"

"He cheated on his wife, and everybody on Coral Island knew it. But this last one was more than a one-night drunken stand, and Sally Jo knew it."

"He was seeing someone regularly while they were separated?"

"Yep. And it was eating up Sally Jo. . . ."

"How did you feel about it?"

Anger flitted across his face. "I think Sally Jo was a fool to even think of going back with him. I heard he gave the other woman up, but once he started drinking again, he'd find another one to replace her down the road. Men like him don't change."

"Maybe so," I said, trying to take everything in. "When did you last see him alive?"

"The morning he died. He was at the marina working on his boat engine. He told me he was going to take Kevin out fishing that afternoon. I said he was crazy to even think about it. The water was too rough. But did he listen? No way."

"Did you have an argument?"

He frowned. "We had words."

"Where were you later that night?"

"At the Fish and Bait Shoppe in Paradisio doing inventory." His mouth thinned into a straight line.

"Did anyone see you there?"

He gave me a direct gaze. "I was closed."

I made a mental note to ask Pete if he'd noticed that Frank was still at the marina. "I've got something I'd like you look at." I reached into my cavernous bag for the fishing fly. After rooting around for a few minutes, I realized that I'd left it back at my Airstream. "Criminy. I forgot it."

"What?"

"A fishing fly. It's very elaborate . . . handmade. Nora Cresswell told me you were an expert on fishing flies, so I thought you might know who made it." I refrained from telling him where I had found it.

"Bring it by my bait store tomorrow, and I'll look at it." His tone was still cautious.

"I'm making coffee." Sally Jo popped her head into the room.

"Thanks. Do you mind if I talk to Kevin? Just to say hi?"

Sally Jo flashed a quick glance in Frank's direction. "I guess it would be okay. He's still all cut up about his daddy, though, so please try not to upset him."

"I won't."

I made my way down the hallway toward Kevin's bedroom. "Kevin?" I knocked on the closed door. "It's Miss Mallie."

"Come in." His voice was muffled.

I entered. The room was dimly lit by a small lamp on his computer desk. Looking around, I took in the aquarium in the corner, Superman-themed bedspread on the twin bed, and model airplane collection on the small dresser. A typical young boy's bedroom. He sat on the floor with a *Chronicles of Narnia* book in his hands. He looked so small and alone, my heart went out to him.

"How ya doing?" I asked.

He looked up at me, his eyes sad—too sad for a boy his age. "Everybody keeps asking me these questions—

like I know what happened to my dad. But I don't. I fell asleep, and when I woke up, he was gone. I don't know *anything*." He stood up and threw the book down.

"I believe you, Kevin." I kept my voice soft and soothing. "Grownups like to have answers, and your dad's falling overboard is kind of a mystery. People want to know why."

He slumped on the bed. "I wish I did know. It would make me feel a whole lot better."

I settled onto the bed next to him. "It wasn't your fault, you know."

"Mr. Billie thinks so." His mouth trembled. "He asked me if I was mad at my dad. If I ever yelled at him." He hung his head. "I did get mad at him sometimes. Still, I wanted him to live here with Mom and me. . . ."

"That's pretty normal to want your dad to live with you. I wouldn't blame you if you were angry with him."

"But Dad told me when we were out fishing that he was moving back in. That he had to take care of something first, but he loved me and Mom." Kevin sniffed.

"Did he explain the 'something'?"

"Nope." Kevin dropped his head into his hands. "I wish I had stayed awake. Then maybe I could've stopped him from falling overboard."

I slipped an arm around him. "You can't think like that, Kevin. Accidents happen, and no one can prevent them."

"My daddy wasn't drunk! I *told* Mr. Billie that." His head snapped up, and he looked at me, tears in his eyes.

"I know," I said in a quiet voice. "You told the truth, and that's so important. But let me ask you something: Is it possible that someone else came aboard the boat? Someone who wanted to . . . uh . . . talk to your daddy?"

His eyes widened as he looked up at me in surprise.

"They would've come up in another boat," I continued, keeping my arm around him.

"I . . . I thought I heard a boat engine!" he exclaimed.

"You did?"

He jerked his head up and down. "It was right before I fell asleep. I thought Dad started up the engines to throw off algae. But maybe it was another boat."

"Maybe so. Did you tell this to Detective Billie?"

"Uh . . . yeah. He didn't say much about it."

I didn't respond, but puzzlement nagged at me. Wouldn't Nick have pushed for more information?

Kevin gazed up at me again with solemn eyes. "It's a good thing I remembered, isn't it?"

I hugged him. "It sure is."

As I let myself out of his room a little while later, I weighed the possibility that another vessel had approached Tom's the night he was murdered. If so, it could've been Jake Fowler or Frank King. Both were experienced boaters, and both had motives to kill Tom. If Nick Billie didn't think so, I'd nudge him along to see it my way—pronto. Anything to clear Kevin.

Feeling pretty good about my hypothesis, I strolled into the living room just in time to see Frank and Sally Jo spring back out of each other's arms. It was more

than a comfort hug. They'd been kissing. Passion-
ately.

Not knowing what to say, I muttered a hasty good-
bye and got the heck out of there.

Oh, yeah. Frank King was a suspect, all right.

Chapter Twelve

It took me about five miles before I could shake off the upset of seeing Sally Jo and Frank wrapped in a passionate embrace. In those moments, she sure hadn't seemed like the grieving widow I'd comforted only two days earlier.

What had happened? Had she found out about Tom's rumored affairs? Or was the whole distraught-widow thing a phony act to disguise something more sinister? Maybe she and Frank had been lovers and plotted together to kill Tom. And where did that leave poor Kevin?

I rubbed a hand across the back of my neck. I was tired. Between hauling Madame Geri around all day, digging up clues about Tom's death, and dealing with his son's sadness, I was worn out.

Being the kind of person that others could count on was exhausting, to say the least. Maybe too much for me. It was so much easier to have only a teacup poodle to answer to.

I pressed down Rusty's accelerator and sped along Cypress Road toward Mango Bay. No cars passed me in the opposite direction, and no one was behind me. I'd learned that when it grew cold, most islanders liked to stay inside. They said your blood thinned when you lived in Florida too long. Not so. I think it was because the basic Florida wardrobe thinned after a few years, and no one had any decent cold-weather gear, except for out-of-date polyesters and velour warm-up suits.

My thoughts drifted back to the fishing fly. I'd take it in to Frank King's bait shop tomorrow and see if I could solicit any information from him. Watch his expression. Decipher his body language.

Then I'd tell Detective Billie about my little piece of evidence.

I realized that I should probably tell Nick about the deceiver first, but I'd promised Wanda Sue that I would protect Kevin and try to find Tom's killer. A promise was a promise.

Wow. I was taking my duties as a friend seriously. Maybe there *were* depths to my character that I hadn't suspected. I was curious to find out—

All of a sudden, Rusty heaved forward. My head jerked backward.

What the heck?

Was the accelerator sticking again?

Thump. My truck lurched again.

No, it wasn't Rusty. Someone had just hit me from behind. I glanced into the rearview mirror and could see only glaring headlights. The vehicle sat a lot higher on the road than my truck, so I couldn't make out anything except the lights. And they were on high beam.

Thump. This time the vehicle hit me harder. My whole body jerked with the impact.

I beeped my horn, rolled down the window, and motioned for it to go around.

The vehicle remained behind me.

Who was it?

I couldn't take the time to find out. I had to get away from whoever it was before they drove me off the road or, worse, flipped me into the ditch.

I floored it. Of course the speed increased only about ten miles per hour, making the grand total of 60 mph. The other vehicle easily closed the distance between us and steadily bore down on me.

Sweat broke out on my forehead as I braced myself for another impact.

The headlights grew larger in my rearview mirror.

"Hold on, Rusty. This is it." My hands tightened around the steering wheel.

Just then another car appeared in the opposite direction, and the vehicle behind me broke off its pursuit.

Realizing this was my chance, I quickly turned off Cypress Road and took a detour through The Mounds—

the highest point on the island, where ancient Caloosa Indians had lived.

I kept a watch in my rearview mirror all the way, but the vehicle disappeared as quickly as it had appeared.

After a few minutes I eased off the gas pedal and drew in a shaky breath.

Had someone just tried to kill me? Me, Mallie Monroe? Disney World dropout and all-around semiflake? Why would anyone want to hurt *me*? Was it the same person who'd sent me the e-mail? Salty Surfer? If so, he had just raised the stakes. Now he wanted me off the case—permanently.

I had a mad desire to call Nick Billie. He wouldn't be at the station at this hour, but I knew there was an emergency number. This was serious. Besides, I needed a strong shoulder and a pair of comforting arms right now.

I flexed my fingers to keep my hands steady. No, I needed to drive back to my Airstream and get my head together. I'd report the incident to Detective Billie tomorrow when I had my wits about me.

Somehow I made it back to the Twin Palms RV Resort in one piece.

My Airstream had never looked so good. Without so much as a glance in the direction of the Wanderlodge, I let myself in. I scooped up Kong and burst into tears.

So much for willpower.

The next morning, I smiled slowly as I realized it was Saturday. Thank goodness I had the morning to sleep in before I had to be at the marina to cover the Autumn Festival fishing tournament. I'd slept fitfully after my brush with death on Cypress Road last night. I kept replaying the scene in my mind, trying to figure out who might've done it.

Unfortunately, I didn't get a good look at the make of the vehicle. Too bad. My car psychology never failed me. In minutes I might've had a handle on who was trying to kill me.

Someone must feel I'm getting too close to finding Tom's killer. And he decided to either scare me—or worse. If I'd hit a telephone pole or flipped, I could've been seriously injured.

I shivered under my old quilt. Kong snuggled in closer to me.

I turned my face into the pillow, not wanting to think any more about my mysterious attacker last night.

Kong tunneled his nose toward me and started to lick my face. After reveling in his canine adoration for a few minutes, I threw the Windbreaker over my pajamas, hooked the leash onto his collar, and swung open the door to my Airstream.

I jumped back with a gasp as I beheld Madame Geri standing there with her trusty bird perched on her shoulder.

"What are you doing here?" I managed to get out.

"Your life is in danger. If you don't act now, you'll be dead."

Kong stared up at Marley and growled low in his throat.

"Come on in." I sighed. "I'll put on a pot of coffee."

I took Kong for a brief walk and then rejoined Madame Geri, who'd parked herself on my sofa and was sipping coffee out of my Epcot stoneware mug. Actually, it was my *only* stoneware mug—courtesy of my tenure at Disney World.

"Make yourself at home," I muttered.

"I had to come," she pronounced, slipping Marley off her shoulder and onto a cushion. This morning she had donned a retro print dress, long sweater, and dangling earrings. The dreadlocks were pinned up with a large bow. *Interesting look.*

"How did you find me?"

"Sandy—she and Jimmy drove me here." She stroked Merlin. "Last night I was finishing Anita's astrological chart, and I felt a cold draft—"

"The wind?" I poured myself a jumbo cup of coffee and slid into a chair a safe distance from that bird.

She shook her head. "My windows were closed. It was a warning from the spirit world. They told me a malevolence was after you."

A tiny chill ran down my spine. "What time did you get this . . . uh . . . warning?"

She looked affronted. "I don't keep clocks in my house. Time is irrelevant."

"Can you estimate?"

"About nine forty-six." She patted the bottom of the sofa, and Kong inched toward her, keeping a canine watch on Marley.

"That's a pretty specific guess."

"I could tell from the position of the stars in the sky. That's much more reliable than anything manmade like a clock." She reached down and stroked Kong's apricot-colored fur. Surprisingly, Kong permitted the intimacy.

"He doesn't usually take to strangers—except Nick Billie," I said, waiting for him to nip at her fingers. But nothing happened.

"We're not strangers, are we?" She smiled down at him, and he wagged his tiny tail.

What that meant, I didn't bother to inquire.

"It's an odd coincidence, but a car almost drove me off the road last night about the time you had your psychic 'warning,' " I revealed reluctantly. I didn't want to encourage Madame Geri's nuttiness, but, then again, I was in no position to ignore her predictions. My life *had* been threatened.

She waved a dismissive hand. "There's no such thing as coincidence. The spirit world wanted me to know that you were in danger."

"Did they tell you who was after me?"

She shook her head. "Not specifically."

I gritted my teeth in frustration. "You can tell the spirits for me that I think they're annoyingly vague. What's the use of all these feelings and visions if they're not going to lead to answers?"

She stroked the top of Kong's head with gentle motions. "Maybe *they're* clear, and it's *we* who cannot understand the truth."

"Mumbo jumbo, if you ask me."

"No, the danger is real, and you need help." She reached into her leather bag and pulled out a silver chain with a tiny ball on it. "Wear this amulet at all times."

I stretched out my hand. She dropped it into my palm and closed my fingers over it. "Marley and I will stick close to you."

Oh, great. I've got a crazy psychic, her beady-eyed bird, and a piece of jewelry to protect me from a murderer. I'd be safer waving a rubber chicken over my head and reciting some kind of protection chant. "We'd better bring in a professional," I said, slipping the necklace around my neck.

"An exorcist?"

"A police officer."

"Oh." She sat back, disappointment etched in her face.

"Let's go see Detective Billie after I take a quick shower." Even though it was the weekend, I didn't need a psychic to tell me that he'd be working. The man practically lived at his workplace, and, right now, that was comforting. He had a murderer loose on the island and wouldn't let up until he'd made an arrest.

"On Saturday?"

"He's there—trust me." I needed him to know that I might be the killer's next target.

By the time I pulled up in front of the police station, I was rethinking my decision to involve Detective Billie. What was I going to tell him? I'd had a threatening e-mail, and the island psychic spooked me after my encounter with an aggressive motorist last night?

He already thought I was a flake. This would probably confirm his suspicions.

Of course, the presence of Madame Geri as my companion didn't help things much. But I didn't know what else to do with her. I was tempted to ask her to wait in my truck, but that seemed unfair, considering the near-freezing temperature.

As we strolled into the station, I caught my reflection in the mirror positioned above the water cooler. I plumped up my freshly washed curls. Okay, so I hadn't taken just a "quick" shower. A little makeup and lip gloss never did a girl any harm. Or wearing a soft green sweater that made my red hair shine like a ripe apple.

Vanity, thy name is Mallie.

Detective Billie appeared in the doorway of his office, arms folded across his broad chest. "Uh-oh, this looks like trouble. Two women and a bird before ten o'clock."

"Hello, Nick. How's life treating you?" Madame Geri inquired.

"Can't complain."

"Mercury goes retrograde in your sign today, so

you're likely to be frustrated. Just wait it out for a few days. . . ."

"Thanks for the advice." One side of his mouth curved upward, but otherwise he had no visible reaction to her prediction.

"Could I talk to you?" I asked, looking at the coffeemaker with dismal realization. Stone cold empty. No delicious aroma emanated from it.

"Sorry, the coffeemaker is broken—something electrical burned out after the last pot. But I've got a Thermos in my office if you'd like a cup."

"Lead the way."

He gestured for me to come into his office. I looked at Madame Geri.

"Marley and I will stay here." She seated herself on the brown leather sofa, settled the parrot on her shoulder, and began to page through a *Time* magazine from 1999. "I need to catch up on world events."

I sent up a silent prayer of relief.

Once in Detective Billie's office, with a lukewarm cup of coffee in my hands, I found myself staring across the desk at his deeper-than-a-starless-night eyes. Everything went blank in my head for a few moments.

"What's up?"

Get it together, girl. "I wanted to report . . . uh . . . an incident last night."

"Such as?" A lazy smile appeared on his face. "You and Madame Geri didn't get rowdy with some bikers at the Seafood Shanty, did you?"

"No." I flashed him a mean look.

"Too bad. I was hoping to see you let loose."

What the heck does that mean? "If I do 'let loose,' you'll be the first to know."

He leaned toward me. "I wouldn't want to have to arrest you."

My heart beat a little fast. *Put the brakes on. You're getting out of your depth.* "I had something more serious to report. Last night, when I was driving back from Sally Jo's house—"

The smile faded. "What were you doing there?"

"Wanda Sue asked me to check on her."

"Did you talk to Kevin?"

I squirmed in my seat but said nothing.

"Mallie, I thought I made it clear that I wanted you to stay out of this case. . . ."

"Kevin and I didn't talk about the murder—not very much, anyway. He said he heard a boat engine—"

"I know. Let me handle this investigation."

"But I think—"

"Don't." He held up a hand.

"Okay. Okay. That isn't why I'm here. Well, maybe it is. . . . I mean, there *was* something sort of odd that occurred while I was at Sally Jo's house. Maybe you wouldn't exactly call it odd. It was sort of unexpected, I guess. At least *I* didn't expect it—"

"Will you come to the point?" he ground out.

"Fine." I raised my chin in defiance. Good old motormouth. It could always be called on to rev up when I least wanted it to.

"I'm waiting." He drummed his fingers on the desk.

"I saw Sally Jo kissing Frank King."

He sat back and placed his hands on the arms of his chair. "They've been friends for years. Went to high school together."

"This wasn't exactly the kind of kiss I'd give to a friend. It was very passionate."

His eyes kindled with interest. "Are you sure that's what you saw?"

"My vision is twenty-twenty, thank you very much."

"Duly noted. Thanks."

"So what do you think? Is it possible Sally Jo and Frank were having an affair?" I took in a deep breath. "That would give Frank motive to kill Tom. He told me that he couldn't stand the way Tom treated his wife. If he loved Sally Jo, he might've wanted to get her husband out of the way."

"Whoa." He held up both hands as if I were a horse ready to bolt. "There's no point in rampant speculating. I deal in facts."

"Is Frank a suspect?"

That muscle began working in his jaw. A sure sign he was debating whether or not to give me information or order me out of his office. "He is a suspect, yes."

"Who else?"

"No comment."

"Jake Fowler? He's got a hair-trigger temper and a mammoth case of resentment over the failure of their clam farm."

"You have been busy." He drilled me with his stare. "No comment."

I threw up my hands. "Has anyone ever told you that you are the most irritating and stubborn man on earth?"

He smiled again—a full-fledged grin. "Has anyone ever told you that you have hair the color of fire?"

My heart revved again, but I wasn't sure if it was in anger or excitement—maybe both. "Many times."

"Then I guess you don't need to hear it again."

Somewhat mollified, I replied, "Compliments are always appreciated."

"Consider it given."

"Well, thanks." I resisted flipping my curls. That would be too much. "There's something else. When I was heading back to the Twin Palms after visiting Sally Jo's, I . . . I . . . was almost driven off the road."

"What?" He snapped to attention as if he'd been doused with a bucket of ice cold water. "Give me the details. And *please* try to be brief."

"I'm always brief."

"Yeah, right." A short bark of laughter erupted from him.

I took a long swig of coffee to fortify myself. "Okay, here's the story. I was driving along Cypress Road, just minding my own business—doing the speed limit, I might add."

He rolled his eyes. "I think that's the maximum speed of your truck, isn't it?"

I ignored the criticism of Rusty. "This vehicle then appeared behind me. It came up really fast and close to my bumper—which, it just so happens, I'd recently replaced." I grimaced. "Anyway, I thought he was going to pass. But instead, he rammed the back of Rusty."

"Rusty?"

"Don't you remember? That's the name of my truck."

"How could I have forgotten? Go on."

"I tried to pull over a little and then to outrun the other vehicle, but it rammed me again. Hard. I almost hit my head on the windshield."

He looked up again, and I thought I detected a swift shadow of concern passing across his face. "Were you hurt?"

I shook my head. "Just shaken up."

"What happened then?"

"I floored it. Of course, as you know, Rusty couldn't go any faster." The image of those glaring headlights closing in on me filled my mind. My breath came in short gasps. "He was going to hit me yet again, but a car appeared in the oncoming lane, and he pulled back. Then I made a quick turn toward The Mounds and lost him."

Detective Billie's face darkened like angry thunderclouds before a sudden tropical rain. "Could you make out the vehicle?"

"No. The headlights were too bright. They filled my rearview mirror. I couldn't see . . ." I snapped my fingers as something clicked in my mind. "Wait—it must've been a big truck or one of those SUVs, because the headlights were high off the road, much higher than a car's. And Frank King drives a big truck." Was it possible that he had tried to hurt me?

"So do ninety percent of the men on this island," he responded dryly. "Including me."

"Oh." I sat back, deflated.

"What about the driver?"

"I couldn't make anyone out." I took in a deep breath. "Do you think it could've been the killer?"

"That's a possibility." He rubbed the back of his neck and leveled a weary glance in my direction. "Anything else?"

I filled him in on the e-mail from the Salty Surfer.

"It was a warning, and you need to heed it." His voice was firm, final. "Stop asking questions about the murder, and let me handle it."

"But I have a story to write, and—"

"You can do that without snooping around for clues about the murder. I'm serious, Mallie. What happened last night should show you that you're way out of your league. Tom's killer might be willing to strike again."

I swallowed hard but remained silent. I debated whether or not to tell him about the fishing fly.

"I know how stubborn you can be. But whatever promise you made to Wanda Sue isn't worth risking your life for." A low, compelling note entered his voice. "Let me do my job."

"What about Kevin? In light of the incident last night, you're not still considering him a suspect, are you?"

"Can't say for sure."

I exhaled in frustration. "What *can* you tell me?"

"I'm pursuing all possible avenues to solve the crime quickly."

"Gee. May I print that?" Sarcasm crackled out of my mouth like a whip.

"Sure."

I drained the rest of my coffee and stood up. At that moment I decided *not* to tell him about the fishing fly—right now. I needed some kind of lead for my investigation, and he wasn't supplying much of anything. The fly was my only clue.

He rose to his feet. "I promise you'll have the exclusive story after I make an arrest."

"That won't satisfy Anita." *Or me.*

"It will have to do."

We stood there, our eyes locked together. I must've been imagining the concern I'd thought I saw in his eyes a few minutes earlier—and the attraction. He was simply angry that I'd interfered in his case. Same old Detective Billie.

"I've gotta go." I turned away.

"Mallie, I don't want you to be hurt—"

I'd already exited his office and slammed the door. At that point Madame Geri held up the outdated magazine.

"Did you know about Monica Lewinsky and President Clinton?"

"Old news."

"He should've confessed at the beginning." She tossed the magazine onto the table and heaved herself off the sofa. "It's bad karma to lie. What goes around comes around."

"Guess so." I held open the door. "We've got to see a man about a fishing fly."

That wasn't bad karma. I hadn't made any promises to Detective Billie. But I had made one to Wanda Sue. And, by golly, I was going to live up to it.

I had cooled down by the time we pulled up in front of Frank's Fish and Bait Shoppe at the Trade Winds Marina. But I was no less determined to find Tom's killer. Telling me I *couldn't* do something was like waving a red flag in front of a charging bull. It inflamed me.

During the drive, Madame Geri had been strangely silent. Ditto for Marley. But after I parked Rusty and was reaching for her rickety door handle, she placed a hand on my arm.

"You can't blame Nick," she said. "He's a wolf—"

"Please, no more New Age junk." I jerked open my door. "Maybe there's a simpler reason: He's a control freak."

"Suit yourself, but I'm rarely wrong." She shrugged and took her hand from my arm. "A wolf can't be tamed—only subdued, at best."

I grabbed my canvas bag and slid out of Rusty, muttering to myself. Madame Geri really needed a big dose of reality. And maybe some intensive therapy to boot.

Before she could fill me in on the details of Detective Billie's lair, I strode into Frank King's shop.

My first impression was that I had wandered into a fisherman's heaven. Dimly lit, the place was packed with every conceivable piece of fishing equipment that had ever been invented. Rods and reels of various sizes and shapes hung everywhere, suspended from the ceiling by neon-colored wires. Whole aisles were devoted to an impressive assortment of flies and hooks. Bait buckets, casting nets, and fishing vests occupied one whole wall. I didn't know where to look first.

Then I spied the signs—wooden plaques to put on your boat that expressed charming sentiments such as: SAIL NAKED or IT'S NOT HOW DEEP YOU FISH BUT HOW YOU WRIGGLE THE WORM. *Classy.*

"Mr. King?"

No answer.

I peered around the fishing vests toward the far end of the store, where an old-fashioned cash register stood.

He wasn't there.

I noticed the back door was open, so I moved toward it. Madame Geri followed close at my heels with Marley on his usual perch.

"Something's up. I feel odd vibrations," she said.

"Just keep that bird quiet," I hissed.

As I approached the door, Frank King suddenly

rushed in carrying a small bundle of rags. He halted, red-faced and flustered, when he saw the two of us. "I . . . I wasn't expecting you this early," he stammered. "You said you'd be by this afternoon."

"I forgot that I had to cover the fishing tournament later today." I tried to make out what was inside the rags. It looked like a paintbrush.

Frank's glance moved from me to Madame Geri. His face took on that reverential look that everyone on the island seemed to adopt the moment they saw her. But there was something else lurking in his demeanor. A twinge of apprehension. Maybe psychics made him nervous. Or maybe he had something to hide.

"I need a few minutes of your time," I said, craning my neck to see what he'd been doing behind the store. The only thing I could make out was his truck parked in the garage behind the building. "Did I catch you in the middle of anything?"

"No . . . uh, sort of." A small paintbrush slipped out of his pile of rags and fell to the floor. Quickly he snatched it up.

"Were you painting?" I asked.

"Yeah." He stuffed the rags into a plastic bag, but not before I saw the paint color streaked across them. Dark blue. The same color as his truck.

"Did you have an accident with your truck, or something?" I asked.

"Not really." He wiped the beaded sweat from his forehead. "I was doing a little touch-up. Someone ran a shopping cart against my passenger door when I was at the grocery store."

Or maybe you damaged the vehicle when you rammed my truck last night. I gave him a hard stare.

Frank went back outside, closing and locking the garage door before I could check out his truck. Then he resumed his position behind the counter. "Now, what about that fishing fly?"

I was tempted to demand a look at his truck, but I'd tip my hand if I did. Instead, I smiled and reached into my bag for the fly. Two could play the cat-and-mouse game. And for once, I felt like the cat and not the mouse.

Chapter Thirteen

I pulled out the fishing fly, protected by layers of tissue. As I unwrapped it, Frank drew in a sharp breath.

"It's incredible." A touch of awe entered his voice, leading me to believe it was the first time he'd ever seen the fly. Or he was an incredibly good actor.

"Madame Geri told me it's a deceiver." *How fitting,* I wanted to add, looking at a man who might be a "deceiver" himself.

He nodded in her direction. "You know your flies, all right."

She plopped herself onto a stool. "Of course I do. I still stay in contact with my father, who was a fisherman."

"Is he on the island?"

"Nope." Madame Geri arranged the folds of her

skirt. "Dad crossed over after he died, but we chitchat every so often."

Frank's eyes widened, and he looked around the room as if to assure himself that Madame Geri's father wasn't hovering around the store. Apparently satisfied, he turned his attention back to the fishing fly. "You don't see flies made with this kind of care too often today. It's hand-made with real feathers. Only master fly builders know how to do this."

"Is there anyone on the island who could make a fly like this?" I kept my tone friendly. "You, for instance?"

He shook his head. "I'm good but not that good." Apparently lost in admiration, he sounded sincere.

"What about Tom Crawford?"

"Tom?" He gave a short bark of laughter. "No way. The most he could do was a standard buzzer."

"A what?"

"Standard buzzer." He reached behind him and grabbed a small plastic packet from the assortment of flies on the wall. "This is one of the easiest flies to make. You just take the hook, twist some seal fur around it, and bind it with your line. Simple. You can make one in fifteen minutes." He pointed at the hook, which appeared to be coated with black fuzz.

"How many types of flies are there?" I studied the buzzer for a few minutes, then transferred my gaze to the multitude of fishing flies on the wall behind Frank.

"There are maybe two dozen patterns—deceivers,

buzzers, nobblers, beetles, nymphs—but each person who makes them can vary the design. So you could have hundreds or even thousands of variations on the basic designs."

"Oh, great," I said without much enthusiasm. My only clue was turning out to be a bust. "So it would be unlikely that I could find out who made this fly? I might be doing a story for the *Observer*." So I stretched the truth a little—okay, maybe a lot.

"Not necessarily." He studied the deceiver in my palm again. "A lot of the unique handmade flies are registered. This pattern—the deceiver—was created by Lefty Kreh. Some people even call them Lefty's Deceivers. But whoever made this fly tweaked the pattern." He touched the fly with reverence. "Notice the real feathers and how the tubing along the shank is hand painted? Beautiful."

My interest was kindled. "You think this one might be registered?"

"I'll check it out."

"Thanks. I'd appreciate it—and my readers will too." I took in a deep breath and asked him point-blank, "Mind if I look at your truck?"

Instantly he stiffened. "Why?"

"I've got to get mine painted, and I was curious about matching colors." Oh, yeah, as if Rusty *had* a discernible color anymore. "How did you find the right paint for the touch-up?"

"The dealer." His mouth pulled tightly in at the corners. "Find the VIN number, and they can get the right shade of paint."

VIN? *Hah.* If Rusty had one, it was long gone. "So, may we see your truck?"

Madame Geri slid off the stool.

"I'd prefer you didn't—not till the paint is dry." Two patches of red appeared on his cheeks. "Could get smudged."

"Suit yourself." I began to rewrap the fly.

All of a sudden Frank snatched it from me.

"Hey, what are you doing?" I grabbed for it. "Give it back."

He stepped back and cradled the deceiver in his hands. "I'll need to keep it so I can sketch the design, research it, maybe even put it out on the Internet."

"I . . . I wanted to do the research myself." The deceiver was my only clue. And I needed to hand it over to Detective Billie. I hadn't exactly decided on *when* I was going to hand the fishing fly over, but I was going to do it.

Frank paled but kept his protective hold on the fly. "Just give me a couple of hours to make some inquiries. Please. It's too beautiful to just let go without trying to find out who made it."

I hesitated. Frank was a suspect. He could destroy the evidence. But short of trying a few Tae Kwon Do maneuvers, I didn't know how I could wrestle it away from him. *Damn.* "Okay. We'll pick it up after the fishing tournament this afternoon. No later. No excuses.

You understand? I've got a witness." I pointed at Madame Geri. "If it 'disappears,' and I see it on eBay, you're going to be in big trouble, mister." I shook my finger at him.

"It'll be here when you return. I promise."

"It had better be," I warned. "By the way, what's your e-mail address?"

"Huh?" He looked blank for a moment. "King52@aol.com."

"Oh." Not that I expected him to say Salty Surfer. Still, I'd thought I might trip him up. But his answer was quick, the information easy to check—not that he couldn't have used Salty Surfer as a temporary address. I hesitated, trying to figure out if I could wrestle him for the fishing fly. Not likely. Still peeved, I finally exited Frank's Fish and Bait Shoppe with Madame Geri and Marley in tow. Once we were back in Rusty, I thumped my head against the steering wheel. "I can't believe I let him take the fly from me like that. Stupid. Stupid. Stupid."

She was silent.

"Nick Billie is going to pitch a fit when he finds out." I turned to her. "Whaddya think? Did the spirits tell you if Frank was guilty or not?"

"He was hiding something—that's for sure." She stroked Marley with an absentminded caress.

"His reaction to the fly seemed genuine," I pointed out with a glimmer of hope that he wouldn't destroy it.

"Maybe."

"But what about the paint on the truck? He sure tried to hide where he did the touch-up."

"True."

I gave a snort of impatience. "Could you be a little more definite? I mean, what's the point of having a psychic with me if you're not getting any vibes?"

She sighed. "Psychic impressions aren't like a water faucet I can turn on and off. When the spirit world thinks the time is right, I'll get 'vibes,' as you call them. And not a moment sooner."

"Fine." I started up Rusty's engine and cranked on the heat. Deceivers and psychic visions aside, I still had another story to cover. The local fishing tournament might not be *Detroit Free Press* front-page headlines, but coverage of it was scheduled for next week's edition. Anita would pitch a nicotine-withdrawal fit if I just blew it off because I was investigating Tom's murder.

Madame Geri and I drove toward the south end of Coral Island, where Sea Belle Isle Point was located. Unlike the north part of the island, where I lived, which boasted a small beach and trailer park, the south tip was much more ritzy.

Canals had been dredged almost a hundred years ago and a large community planned, called Sea Belle Isle Point on the Gulf. Needless to say, the community never expanded beyond a few hundred people—maybe because no one wanted to live in a place with a name that long. Or maybe because the area could only be accessed by ferry at that time. Whatever the reason, Sea Belle Isle

Point had languished until about ten years ago, when a small causeway was built and wealthy tourists "discovered" the appeal of direct Gulf-access canals.

Fancy-schmancy "old Florida" houses went up, along with a clubhouse and marina. The Sea Belle Isle Point inhabitants kept themselves separate from the rest of the islanders, except for occasional charity events where they could bestow their magnanimous wealth on the community. The fishing tournament was one of those occasions. Money raised from the event went to the Coral Island Elementary School—not that any of the Sea Belle Isle Point kids attended it. Their mothers drove them into town to exclusive private schools, thank you very much.

As I parked Rusty in the country club parking lot, I noted the Lexus to my right and the Mercedes to my left. I patted Rusty's faded plastic dashboard, murmuring, "Don't let them intimidate you, buddy. Could they pull an almost five-thousand-pound Airstream?"

I gave my truck another pat and turned off the engine. It backfired with a loud burst of sooty exhaust. Madame Geri said nothing, but the significant arching of her eyebrows spoke volumes.

"Rusty's just clearing his throat." I jerked on the door handle, which promptly fell off. Screwing it back in, I managed to open the door and get out before anything else could happen. Rusty needed body work, especially now that the bumper was messed up again. When I got a few paychecks ahead next year, I intended to take him for a spring "spruce up" at the body shop in town. If he could hold out until then . . .

As we headed toward the clubhouse, I zipped up my windbreaker and hunched my shoulders. The sun had finally peeped through the blanket of gray clouds, but the temperature hadn't warmed up much. A teeth-chattering wind still roared in off the Gulf, bringing a wind-chill factor that seemed to penetrate my best attempts to layer against the cold.

"A bit nippy, huh?" Madame Geri said, clutching her cape around her like a protective tent. Even Marley had his wings drawn in tightly against the cold. I guess the bird wasn't that dumb after all.

I muttered something unintelligible and kept moving toward the prospective heat of the clubhouse. Once inside, I realized it wasn't much warmer there. The French doors at the far end were wide open, so people could move back and forth between the building and the fishing pier directly behind. A huge banner hung from the ceiling, saying *Welcome, Coral Island Hookers*. Catchy. I reached for my Official Reporter's Notepad. "I've got to do some interviews and snap a few photos. Catch you later."

She nodded and moved off in the direction of the refreshments table. I headed out toward the pier.

Lots of islanders milled around the docks, many with fishing poles in hand. One of the guys who played guitar on Friday nights at the Seafood Shanty twanged away under a palm tree, and the smell of sizzling seafood wafted out of the covered tent.

"Hi, Mallie," Sandy said as she approached with Jimmy at her side, both of them wearing olive drab fishing vests. I spied a price tag peeping out of the armhole of hers. I smiled.

"Jimmy, your mom is around here somewhere." I scanned the room but didn't see her.

"She's probably going to set up somewhere to do readings." His arm slid around Sandy's shoulders. "She can't be in a place for five minutes without people wanting to have their fortunes told. It's an occupational hazard."

"Must be like doctors always being badgered for free medical advice." I tried to keep the amusement out of my voice. "You guys fishing for prizes?"

"You bet." Jimmy held up his pole proudly. "I won second place in the saltwater fly-fishing division last year. I intend—"

My interest immediately perked up. "You mean people will be fly-fishing today? In saltwater?"

"Sure. You can catch saltwater fish on flies just as easily as freshwater. Maybe even better. I like using a thirty-yard line, a black Lab deceiver—"

"A deceiver? You use one of those?" My voice grew excited.

"Everyone does. They work so well here. Most of the islanders make special flies for the tournament." He held up a fly with black and gray feathers. Even to my untrained eye, it didn't appear to be nearly as complicated as the one I'd found on Tom's boat.

"You and Jimmy have fun. . . . I've got a story to do." Sprinting past them, I stepped onto the pier. Excitement kindled inside of me. I had a prime opportunity to preview all the islanders' fishing flies while appearing to work on my article. If the murderer were here today, I might be able to pinpoint him by his fly. I grinned to myself. *All right, keep it clean, Mallie. His* fishing *fly.*

I strolled toward a group of fishermen at the end of the pier. Jake Fowler wasn't among them. I took a few photos, asked some questions for my article, getting people's reactions to the tournament, and managed to scope out their flies. Fishing flies, of course.

Nothing but run-of-the-mill stuff.

I started to make my way back to the shore when I spied a young woman with a group of kids clamoring around her. It was Beverly from the school. I'd recognize that lovely gold hair anywhere. Unfortunately, the rest of her appearance still screamed "schoolteacher." A long black skirt, plaid coat, and Mary Janes completed the picture of Mary Poppins in the twenty-first century. As I approached her, I noticed the expert flick she gave to her fishing pole, launching her fly way out into the water.

"I can tell you've done your share of fishing," I said.

She turned around and looked blank for a few moments.

"Mallie Monroe, from the *Observer*. Remember I came to cover the jump-rope story at the elementary school?"

Recognition dawned in her eyes. "Oh, yes, of course. I knew I'd seen you somewhere. It's just that I deal with so many students and their parents that sometimes I sort of forget who I've talked to."

"Sure." I couldn't make out what kind of fly was on the end of her line. It looked larger than some of the other ones I'd seen today. "Since I've got you here, I might as well get a quote for my article."

"Miss . . . miss!" A little boy with large brown eyes and hair that flopped over his forehead was pulling on her coat. "My line is all messed up."

"Never a dull moment. Just a sec." She set her pole down, took his, and with a few deft movements untangled his line and handed it back to him. "Here, go join Robby and the other boys."

Once again I was impressed with her fishing acumen. I decided I had to get a look at her fly. I don't know how or why she could be connected to Tom, but anything was possible.

One boy from the group waved at me. It was Kevin. I waved back. Then I frowned when I saw that Robby Fowler was also in the little group. "It's nice to see Kevin out here with his—"

"Buddies. Yes, I know." A cloud of doubt settled over the delicate oval of her face. "But to tell you the truth,

I'm a little concerned. The other boys in his class have heard about Tom's death and the rumors that it was . . . murder." She stumbled over the last word as if it were an obscenity. "They're upset and scared."

"Of Kevin?"

She picked up her fishing pole again. "I'm afraid so."

"They don't actually think he'd—"

"Hurt them?" she cut in again.

I glared at her. One, because she was painting Kevin in a bad light. And, two, because she seemed genetically unable to let me finish a sentence.

"I hate to say this about one of my own students, but I'm a little nervous around him myself."

"That's ridicu—"

"Is it? I've seen Kevin's temper in the classroom. He's easily frustrated and takes it out on his classmates. I've tried to work with him, knowing his parents were separated, but he's been sent to detention almost a dozen times over the last month alone."

"What for?" That odd, protective feeling rose up inside me again. At the ripe old age of twenty-eight, was I finally becoming maternal? Nah. It couldn't be. I didn't particularly like kids. I just hated seeing anyone get picked on.

"Fighting with the other boys. He's got quite a temper, and I've been concerned that he might injure one of his classmates." She clucked her tongue in an irritating manner that reminded me of my old schoolteachers, who were always comparing me to my straight-A, never absent, always perfect sibling. "One time he hit a boy on the head with a paperweight."

A tiny alarm went off in the back of my mind. "Did you tell the police?"

"Of course. I had to."

No wonder Detective Billie still considered Kevin a suspect. A hot-tempered, violent boy on a boat with his dad who'd deserted him. I had to admit, it didn't sound good even to me.

"Did you call in the school counselor—" I began.

"Killer!" a boy screamed. "Daddy killer!"

"No. No. No!" another boy yelled back.

I turned toward the group of boys in time to see Kevin knock down Robby Fowler, then rain punches on his face in a fit of rage.

"I'll kill you!" Kevin exclaimed.

Chapter Fourteen

"**B**oys, stop that!" Beverly shouted and clapped her hands. They ignored her.

"Hit him! Hit him!" the other boys clamored. I wasn't sure if they were encouraging Kevin or Robby, but I realized that one of them was going to get hurt.

I pushed past the circle of boys and reached for Kevin. But Jake Fowler got there first. He pulled Robby back by the hood of his jacket. I slipped an arm around Kevin to keep him in check. His breathing was ragged, his whole body shaking.

"What's the matter with you, boy?" Jake exclaimed. "Haven't I told you about fighting?"

Robby's face was flushed. "But you're the one who told me Kevin's dad was a no-good—"

"That's not the point. You don't rag on a boy when

181

he's down. He just lost his father. Cut him some slack."

I almost gasped. Was this Jake Fowler? He actually seemed to be showing some sympathy for Kevin.

"But, Dad—"

"It's time for you to go home." He grabbed Robby's fishing pole. "Sorry 'bout this." He looked at me rather than Beverly. "He'll be grounded, I can tell you."

Robby began to cry.

Jake hustled him away from the group, chastising him every step of the way. The other boys turned back to their fishing poles, whispering among themselves.

"Are you okay, Kevin?" I squatted down to his level.

"Yeah." The anger had faded from his face. Now he just looked embarrassed. "Sorry."

"It's okay that—"

"No, it's not okay," Beverly cut in, her voice at a shrill pitch that sounded like nails scraping across a chalkboard. "Kevin, how many times have I talked to you about practicing self-control? You simply *cannot* continue hurting other children. If you do, the principal will have to remove you from the school. Is that what you want?"

"No, miss."

"I didn't think so." She folded her arms across her flat chest. Her face took on a pinched quality that offered a preview of what she would look like in twenty years. It wasn't pretty.

"You don't even know who started the fight." I rose to my feet. "It could've been any of the other boys."

"Robby? Maybe so. But Kevin was the one who had him down, pummeling his face. That is totally unacceptable."

"Yes, miss," he mumbled.

"What's going on here?" Detective Billie strode up to us, looking big and handsome in his jeans and black leather jacket.

"Oh, Nick, thank goodness you're here," she tittered. The pinched look vanished, replaced by a coy, mincing smile. *Ick*. That was even worse. Not that I was jealous. Far from it.

"The boys just had a little ruckus, and—" I began.

Beverly brushed aside my comments and blurted out, "Kevin had Robby Fowler down on the dock and was beating him senseless."

"Oh, come on. It wasn't like that—"

"Poor Robby was saved in the nick of time by his father," she continued.

"Okay, I'll take it from here." Detective Billie glanced down at Kevin from what must've seemed a great height to the young boy. "Whaddya say we go get a hot chocolate and chat?" he proposed, his voice firm.

"Okay." Kevin pointed at me. "Can she come too?"

His eyes caught and held mine. "Sure. If we can keep her from talking too much."

Beverly laughed and started to say something, but

then her cell phone rang. She pivoted on her heel, chatting away on the phone, and strolled toward her students with a saucy sway to her hips. *Spare me.*

"Thanks a lot, Nick." I gave an affronted snort. "You can pick up the tab for the hot chocolates."

Kevin and I trooped inside. Detective Billie followed a few minutes later after a brief stop at the concession stand.

We found a table set off in an alcove by itself and pulled up a couple of chairs. Kevin immediately grabbed for his hot chocolate. He downed almost half of it in one long swallow, leaving a little brown mustache over his upper lip.

Detective Billie dabbed at the boy's mouth with a napkin. "Now, Kevin, tell me what happened out there on the dock."

Kevin hung his head low on his chest. "I'm sorry."

"I know you are, but I still need some details," he continued.

"I was minding my own business—just fishing, that's all, I swear. The other boys didn't say much to me, but that's okay. I didn't want to talk to them neither." His defensive tone told the opposite story. "Anyways, Robby came up and started boasting. Said he was gonna catch the biggest fish. Stuff like that. I ignored him. But then he pushed me and said he wanted my fishing spot. I still didn't do anything. Honestly."

I didn't respond, but I believed him. Detective Billie sipped his hot chocolate in silence. I did likewise.

"Then he started saying things. Like my dad was a no-good so-and-so who cheated his dad. And that nobody would . . . miss him." Kevin sniffed and swiped at the film of tears that threatened to spill onto his cheeks.

"And that's when you hit him?" Nick inquired gently.

Kevin nodded.

I pressed my lips together in a tight line to keep from adding my two cents' worth. Who wouldn't have struck out in anger? Kevin had been pushed beyond what a young boy could take.

"I get the picture." Detective Billie sat back in his chair, studying Kevin. "It's tough when the other guys taunt you. Trust me, I know. A lot of kids used to make fun of me because I was half white and half Indian—"

"Did you get mad?" Kevin asked.

"Sure. And it hurt inside. But you've got to be bigger than they are. Nothing is ever going to be fixed through violence. That only breeds more violence. Losing control like that makes them win every time."

"Yes, sir," Kevin said in a small voice.

"After you tell your mom what happened, she and I can talk about getting you some anger-management counseling at school."

Kevin's mouth drooped. "Do I have to?"

"Yeah, you do."

At that point, Wanda Sue swept in like a mini maternal tornado, arms flapping, high heels clattering. "Kevin, are you all right? I heard Robby Fowler and you was in a brawl." She folded him into her arms for a quick hug.

Then she scanned him and patted him down. "No black eyes, no broken bones."

"I'm fine, Nana." Kevin wriggled like a fresh-caught fish. "It was just a fist fight."

"Boy, you're gonna give your nana a heart attack." She placed a hand against her ample chest. "No fighting. Haven't your momma and I told you that often enough?" She looked at Detective Billie. "Are you gonna arrest him for disturbing the peace?"

I heard Kevin draw in a quick gasp.

Detective Billie's mouth quirked, but he kept his expression stern. "We'll let him off this time with just a warning. But have Sally Jo call me. We need to talk."

Wanda Sue drew her palms together in a prayerlike posture. "Thank you, Nick. I'll have her call you Monday morning." She reached down to take her grandson's hand. "Let's go home."

Kevin started to go. At the last minute he turned back toward Detective Billie. "I'll tell my mom about the fight when I get home."

"Good idea. It's best she hear the details from you first."

The boy nodded and shook hands with Detective Billie.

I observed this solemn exchange but waited until Kevin had left before I said anything. "Don't you think you were a bit hard on him?"

"Nope." He drank some more of his hot chocolate,

looking rather cute with a faint foamy mustache on his upper lip.

"Boys do that kind of thing all the time. That's what they do. They fight," I pointed out as a took a long swig of the hot beverage. It wasn't coffee, but it still chased away the chill.

"An occasional fight is okay. But Kevin's temper has gotten out of control. Beverly Jennings has called me several times over the last couple of months. It started with the usual kind of thing—pushing and shoving on the playground. But then the incidents escalated." Nick frowned, wiping his upper lip clean.

My eyes narrowed in suspicion as I set my cup down. "Has something happened to implicate Kevin?"

He set his cup next to mine. "Tests showed that Tom was hit in the back of the head with an oar."

My nerves tensed. "Did you find any . . . fingerprints?"

"Several. They were all smudged." He toyed with his cup. "Except for Kevin's."

"But . . . but that could mean anything." I placed my hand on his arm. "Kevin could've picked up the oar to . . . to shove off from the dock. Or he might have . . . uh . . . put it into the water to check on the depth. Or maybe—"

"I know. All of those are possibilities. That's the reason he's not under house arrest."

"He didn't murder his father. I'm sure of it."

Nick's silence spoke volumes. He had doubts. He

might be doing everything he could to question other suspects, but Kevin wasn't in the clear. Not by a long shot.

I withdrew my hand. "Have you questioned Jake Fowler or Frank King about Tom's death?"

His face immediately shuttered down as if a shade had been drawn over his features. "I might have."

I plunged on. "Frank King had the flimsiest of alibis the night Tom was killed—said he was at his Fish and Bait Shoppe doing inventory. But what about Jake?"

"You stopped by his store this morning?" he inquired.

"Uh . . . yeah."

"Are you holding something back? If it pertains to the investigation, you'd better tell me pronto."

Oh, darn it anyway. He'd find out eventually, and if it wasn't from me, he'd probably throw me in jail. Reluctantly I filled him in about finding the piece of evidence on Tom's boat.

His nostrils flared in anger. "Just when were you going to tell me about the fishing fly?"

"Today." I hedged. "That's why I came here—and to cover the fishing tournament for the *Observer*, of course and—"

"That's bull, and we both know it," he cut in, slamming both arms onto the table. "Where is the fly right now?"

"Frank snatched it from me."

"What?" He now looked more incredulous than angry. That was a good sign. Wasn't it?

"I went there just to get information about the fly on the pretext that I was doing a side story to go with the fishing tournament. But he seemed so awed by it, I let my guard down. Then, before I knew it, he took it from me, saying he wanted to research who might've made it. At that point there was nothing much I could do. At least I had a witness—Madame Geri saw the whole thing." I tried to put my motormouth into Park, but it resisted. "Sorry. I know I messed up, but I thought the fly might lead me—I mean *you*—to the killer, and—"

"Enough already." He thumped the table again with one hand. "How do you know he isn't at this very moment destroying the evidence?"

"Good question." I swallowed hard. It was becoming increasingly difficult to defend my position in the face of his wrath. "Instinct, I guess. Something told me when I showed him the fly that he hadn't made it. He looked too entranced by the thing. If you could've seen the look on his face, you'd know what I mean. He touched it as if it were a holy object or something. Granted, I thought it was excessive, but would he have done that if he'd seen it before—"

"All right. All right." He raised his eyes upward, and I could hear him counting under his breath. Did I make him that crazy? I smiled inwardly. At least it was a reaction.

"So you see, I don't think he could've made it," I finished with a flourish. "But I'm not totally dismissing him as a suspect."

He finished counting and dropped his head into his hands.

"Detective Billie? Nick? Are you all right?" I tapped him on the elbow.

"I'm fine, thank you," he mumbled into his hands, drawing his arm away from me as if my touch burned him.

I guess I did make him that crazy. Poor man. "Would it help if we drove to the marina and picked it up?" I offered in my sweetest voice.

"No." His head jerked up. "Yes. What I mean to say, is, *I'll* get it. Oh, hell, now I'm talking like you."

I tried for a posture of affronted dignity. "There's nothing wrong with the way I talk."

"Except you never stop. Oh, *pardon me*"—his tone turned a bit nasty—"you do conveniently cut the chatter when you're interfering with *my* investigation."

"If I don't come with you, you won't be able to tell which fly was the one I found on Tom's boat." I smiled.

He opened his mouth as if to say something else but then clamped his lips shut. A short nod sufficed.

We both stood up, and as if on cue, Madame Geri tottered toward our table.

"Are we leaving?" she asked, juggling a steaming cup of java and a dish of smoked mullet. Marley remained on his usual perch atop Madame Geri's shoulder.

"*We* are leaving. Mallie and I have to make a stop—"

"On official police business," I cut in.

He groaned.

"I figured as much." She cocked her chin at an angle

and wagged her head. "I was finishing up Old Man Brisbee's Tarot card reading—"

"The coot who pinches my butt?" I pointed at my derriere. "I hope you saw nothing but bad luck in his future."

"Nope. Sorry to say, he had the sun card in his reading. That's always a good sign."

"Wouldn't you know?" I muttered in disgust.

"Ladies, as fascinating as this discussion is, I've got an investigation to handle." He gestured toward the front door with both hands. "Can we move along?"

"Madame Geri too?" I inquired. "I'm supposed to drop her back at the *Observer* office."

"Why not?" He sighed. "We'll swing by on our way off the island."

We trooped out to his Ford F-150 truck parked next to a deep blue Acura 2.5 TL. Unlike Rusty, Detective Billie's truck was a late model. Shiny black exterior. Four doors with a full back seat. Spanking-new tires. I didn't need to invoke my degree in Advanced Car Psychology to tell me that his truck was an extension of himself—dark and powerful.

Once we settled in, Madame Geri in the rear seat with Marley, me in the front with Detective Billie, I sat back and enjoyed the ambiance of a new vehicle. I'd never trade Rusty. Honestly. But it was nice to feel the comfort of a well-padded bucket seat once in a while.

"Are you heading to Frank King's Fish and Bait Shoppe?" Madame Geri asked once we were under way.

"Yes," Nick replied. "But you're not coming along."

"Suit yourself." She folded her hands in her lap. "But I had a bad vibe a little while ago when finishing up Old Man Brisbee's reading. A shadow passed across Frank's aura."

Detective Billie and I locked glances.

"Change of plan. Hold on tight." His expression darkened with an unreadable emotion as he rammed down the gas pedal.

Chapter Fifteen

Detective Billie covered the short distance from Sea Belle Isle Point to the marina at Paradisio in record time. In spite of my low-level anxiety, I couldn't help but notice the magnificent acceleration of his truck. After so many years of driving with a maximum speed of 55 mph, it was a treat to experience true horsepower. I had truck envy. I admit it.

As we pulled into the parking area in front of the Fish and Bait Shoppe, Nick cut the engine. It instantly shut down, with none of the chugging and lurching that happened every time I tried to turn off Rusty's ancient six-cylinder engine. More truck envy.

"Both of you stay here," he ordered as he removed the latch that held his gun in its holster.

My eyes widened, and I nodded mutely.

He exited the truck and strode toward the front door of Frank's store. After he disappeared inside, Madame Geri and I exchanged glances and reached for our respective door handles.

"Is Marley an attack bird?" I asked as we climbed out of the truck and crept toward the building.

"He can hold his own." She lifted one of his spindly legs and exhibited three-inch talons.

For once I felt comforted by those mean-looking claws. They could do some major damage and then some. I pointed at the front window. We both peered through the hazy glass.

"Can you see anything?" Madame Geri whispered.

"No, it's sort of dark inside. Or maybe the window is just dirty. I can't tell." I tiptoed toward the door and slipped inside, Madame Geri and Marley at my heels.

It took my eyes a few moments to adjust to the dim light that barely illuminated the aisles. The overhead fluorescents were out, making it seem almost like early evening. But a glow emanated from the back of the store. We moved toward it. Unfortunately, along the way I tripped over a plastic tackle box, causing its contents to spill all over the floor.

"Damn." I halted.

But Madame Geri kept moving. She rammed into my back, causing me to crash into a fishing pole rack. As the poles fell with a clatter, Marley let out a shrill squawk, and Madame Geri choked back a shriek.

"Shh!" I hissed, and I stepped over the jumbled poles. "Be careful of—" I broke off. Rapid, staccato footsteps were moving in our direction. "Oh, no. Get a weapon, arm yourself." I scooped up a pole and held it out like a sword. Madame Geri picked up a fishing net.

The footsteps drew closer. I closed my eyes for a brief moment and tightened my grip on the pole.

"Didn't I tell you to stay in the truck?" Detective Billie demanded as he rounded a row of life vests, flashlight in one hand, gun in the other.

Relief flooded through me. "We . . . we were cold." *Lame. Totally lame.* "And worried—"

"So you decided that the best thing to do was to come barging in here and knock down every item in the store? Good thinking." Irony threaded through his voice, more leaden than the heavy-duty lures Frank had on a $1.89, two-for-one special. "Will you put down that stupid pole and help me? Frank's been hurt."

"I knew it." Madame Geri tossed the fishing net to the floor. "Auras never lie."

Detective Billie stared at her for a few moments. "I called 911. They should be here in a few minutes." He turned and strode toward the far end of the store.

"What happened to Frank?" I jogged in his wake.

"Looks like someone knocked him on the back of the head with a small anchor, then held his face down in the bait tank with a fishing net." Nick's voice turned grim as he kept walking. "He's lost a lot of blood but somehow survived."

"Sounds . . . similar to Tom's murder. Trauma to the head," I managed to get out breathlessly.

We rounded the counter, and I stopped in my tracks. Frank lay sprawled on the floor, facedown next to the tipped over bait tank. A thick white nylon fishing net was wound around his head, stained with blood. "Shouldn't we try to stop the bleeding?" I swallowed hard, eying the anchor, also streaked with blood. I pressed my nails into the palms of my hands to keep from fainting.

"That's what I was about to do when you showed up. I wasn't sure if it was you or the assailant." He handed me a towel. "Take this and apply pressure to the wound."

I froze. Was I going to have to touch that red spot on the back of his head?

"I don't have time for you to be squeamish. Either use the towel or give it to Madame Geri." He gently pushed aside the fishing net, so I had a clear view of the wound.

Stay strong. I refused to let that half-baked phony psychic show me up. I knelt next to Frank's motionless body and gingerly set the towel on his head.

"Pressure. Apply pressure!" Nick ordered with some urgency.

I took a deep breath and pressed down on the wound. A deep red stain immediately appeared on the cloth. I turned my face away and continued to bear down on Frank's head.

"Don't touch anything else. I'm going to secure the premises." Nick moved away, gun and flashlight still in hand.

I wanted to scream, "Don't leave us!" But I knew he had to do his thing. If whoever did this to Frank was still hanging around, we might be in danger.

"Frank will survive," Madame Geri said.

I looked up at her. Her eyes were closed. "How do you know?"

"The spirit world just told me. It's not his time yet."

"I don't suppose they could give us a clue as to who did it?"

She was silent for a few moments. Then her eyes snapped open. "Nope."

"You see, that's why I could never be a real psychic. Sure, I worked at a psychic hotline, but that was a sham. The thing that bothers me with the spirit world, as you call it, is, if you really need specific answers to questions, you never seem to get them." My motormouth was up and running. I was scared and nervous, the two conditions that revved my mouth into overdrive. "If the spirits can't give you accurate data, what use are they? I'd be so frustrated if I were you. . . . It's like being semi-starved. They throw you some crumbs just to whet your appetite, but when it comes down to the whole enchilada, you never—"

"What enchilada?" she interrupted, her forehead wrinkling in puzzlement.

"I'm not talking about food." Tears sprang to my eyes. This whole scene was intense, and I was rapidly losing control. I had my hand on a wound, and a man's life hung in the balance. Me—the person who closed her eyes when the vet gave Kong his booster shots. How could I be in this situation? I should be home in my Airstream, trying to figure out whether I wanted to have tuna or macaroni and cheese for dinner. "Where's that ambulance anyway? Don't they know Frank could die if they don't get here soon?"

Madame Geri placed a hand on my shoulder and spoke in a quiet voice. "It's okay. You're doing everything you can."

Much to my surprise, her composure seemed to settle my rising panic. I blinked back the tears and focused on stopping the bleeding. I pressed down hard on the wound, no longer averting my eyes from the red blotch. I *was* doing something. Frank King was going to live if I had anything to do with it.

At that moment, sirens approached. In less than two minutes paramedics rushed into the store, strapped Frank to a gurney, and hooked him up to an IV.

"Is he going to make it?" I asked one of young guys who was bandaging Frank's wound.

"Can't tell. He's lost a lot of blood. But we'll do everything we can." His hands moved deftly, covering the wound in a matter of seconds. Then he and another guy wheeled Frank outside.

Madame Geri and I moved to the front of the store and watched them put Frank into the ambulance. Nick oversaw the whole thing, speaking a few words to the paramedics before they left.

When they drove off, I kicked a wooden decoy out of the way and leaned against a wall, suddenly aware that my legs were shaking. Remarkably, Madame Geri seemed unfazed by the whole series of events, though Marley appeared somewhat agitated. "I can't believe you're so calm," I commented with some envy.

"Once the spirit world let me know that Frank was going to live, I knew there was nothing to get upset about." She stroked Marley's turquoise feathers and murmured soothing words.

I took in the serene expression on Madame Geri's face. Maybe she wasn't quite so half-baked, after all. There was something to be said about having a pipeline, whether real or perceived, to the spirit world. I was willing to concede that, unlike my fellow practitioners at the psychic hotline, she did cherish a true faith in her own brand of New Age nuttiness. And, in this world, that practically amounted to sainthood.

Detective Billie came bursting back onto the scene, his gun in its holster. "You didn't touch anything— especially that anchor—did you?"

"Gee, that's a nice way of saying thank you." My legs had settled down to minor tremors.

He looked at me blankly for a few moments. "Sorry— thanks." He flipped on the overhead lights.

"Don't knock yourself out." Under the glare of the fluorescents, I noticed that my hands were stained with Frank's blood. That faint feeling passed over me again.

"Here, take this." Nick grabbed a couple of rags out of a barrel that was positioned near the door, then sprinkled paint thinner over them. Rubbing my hands, he removed the redness.

"Better?" he questioned, tossing the rags out the front door.

"Sort of."

"Mallie, keep it together, okay?" His voice deepened in concern.

"I'm trying."

"Concentrate on your yin, not your yang," Madame Geri chimed in.

"Take a few deep breaths," Nick continued. "Nice and slow." He moved in closer and stroked my back with a gentle touch. "That's it."

I allowed myself to lean on him while my breathing returned to normal. Several aromas assailed my senses. Woodsy aftershave. Leather. Paint thinner. My head was spinning.

"Look, Mallie, I need you. . . ." He paused, grasping both my arms.

"Yes?" I asked, breathless.

"To identify the fishing lure you gave Frank. Do you remember what it looked like?"

"I . . . uh . . . I think so." I felt an instant's squeezing hurt inside. A pang. Or maybe it was still a tremor. I didn't know. My wits were totally scattered at that point.

"Good." He led me toward the back of the store. As

we moved away from Madame Geri, I motioned her to follow us.

"Who do you think attacked Frank?" I asked as we passed the rows and rows of island Reeboks.

"Someone who thought Frank had a piece of evidence that could incriminate them."

"Tom's murderer?"

"Exactly."

"So the fishing fly *is* important to the case," I continued. "It could point to the killer."

He nodded. "That's why it would've helped if you'd turned it over to me when you found it." His fingers tightened around my hand. It was *not* gentle. More like a punishing vise.

I winced.

Once we reached the long counter that stretched almost the entire length of the back wall, Nick released my hand. It dropped to my side, cold and bereft.

"Do you see the fly anywhere in that pile?" He pointed at a large assortment of fishing flies scattered across the counter.

I rummaged through deceivers, buzzers, and nymphs, seeking the distinctively colored feathers of the fly I'd found on Tom's boat.

"No luck." I held up a lemon drop deceiver. "It looked like this, but the feathers were real, the shank black, and the color more of a chartreuse."

"That helps a lot," he muttered.

"I'm doing the best I can," I tossed the yellow deceiver back onto the pile. "Do you think Frank's attacker took it?"

"That would be my best guess." His mouth turned down.

"What about all these books?" I picked up one of the several thick books lying open next to his computer. I noticed its screen was lit up—the source of that glowing light I'd seen before. Frank had left his computer on. "Looks like he was also checking Internet sites."

Detective Billie nodded. "He was probably researching the fly in both places, trying to find out who might've made it."

I glanced at the book in my hand. *The Comprehensive History of Fishing Flies*. That sounded like a best seller. I picked up another one. *Fishing Flies for the Discriminating Saltwater Fisherman*. "Wow. Just the kind of sizzling book I'd like to read on a Saturday night."

"That's what I was hoping you'd say." He stacked two more books into my arms. I staggered slightly under their weight. *So much for the tender moment.* "While I check out his computer, you can go through these books," he continued.

"You're kidding, right?" I struggled to keep the stack straight.

He cocked one eyebrow. "I think it's the least you can do, considering you were withholding crucial evidence in a murder investigation."

"You really know how to hit a girl where it hurts, don't you?"

"Just doing my job, ma'am." He bowed his head.

I glared at him.

"There was anger in this room," Madame Geri said, setting Marley on a merchandise shelf. She was running her hands up and down her arms. "No, more than that. Anger drove him, but also fear. He's afraid you're getting too close—wants to protect himself at all costs."

"You said 'him.' A man?" Detective Billie rubbed his chin. I noticed the five o'clock shadow appearing along his jawline. All at once, he looked tired.

"Maybe." She raised both hands and turned her eyes upward. I could only presume she was trying to force an answer from the "other world." "The spirits are silent," she said with a sigh.

Madame Geri said no more. She didn't need to. The atmosphere in the Fish and Bait Shoppe turned deadly quiet. My motormouth was lodged in permanent Park. Detective Billie had become as silent as the grave. Now why had I suddenly thought of that image?

Whether Madame Geri really was conversing with spirits or not was moot. She had stated an obvious truth: It was very possible that Tom's killer had attacked Frank King and might strike again.

Chapter Sixteen

A scant few hours later, I was ensconced safely in my Airstream, huddled under the electric blanket with Kong snuggling next to me. It wasn't supposed to go below forty tonight, but my heater had decided to grant me only a few puffs of tepid air. I didn't know if the thermostat had finally gone on the blink, or what, but I couldn't get Pop Pop Welch in to look at it until morning. At his age, bedtime came right after the six o'clock news.

I fluffed up my pillows and propped up *The Comprehensive History of Fishing Flies* on my stomach, holding it in place with my drawn-up knees.

Reading this tome was the last thing I felt like doing, but Detective Billie had shamed me into it. Once he had dropped Madame Geri at her house and me back at Sea Belle Isle Point, I'd cranked up Rusty and headed right to Mango Bay to get started on my Saturday night reading. He was heading back to Frank's store to analyze the data on Frank's computer.

Much as I wanted to know who had made the deceiver, I'd found a hundred things to do before I actually got down to opening the book. Shakespeare it wasn't, but I'd finally cracked it open.

Sighing, I started scanning the pages again. About ten pages later, my eyes started drooping. I forced my lids open. I *had* to read this book.

Unbidden, images of Tom's body splayed against the mangroves and Frank lying on the floor in a pool of his own blood flooded through my mind.

I shuddered. But at least I was wide awake.

I flipped back to the Table of Contents and found the chapter on deceivers. Locating the section, I read the introduction to Bernhard "Lefty" Kreh, the man who'd created the deceiver. From all the hyperbole, you would think he was the god of the fishing flies. Or, as they so quaintly put it, *Lefty Kreh, the Michaelanglo of Master Builders*.

I yawned.

I scanned the descriptive pages that explained why the deceiver was one of the best-known patterns in saltwater fly fishing.

Highly adaptable, this pattern can be used to imitate

a specific species of bait fish, a category of bait fish, or a general bait fish imitation.

So versatile, deceivers can be taken anywhere!

A durable tie, it can take the punishment of big-game fish.

It's aerodynamic!

I yawned again.

This was a going to be a long night.

Scanning the next twenty pages, I was treated to further information on Lefty—Lefty's life story, Lefty's contribution to the wonderful world of fly fishing, Lefty's later years, Lefty's master fly building disciples . . .

I halted.

Was it possible that the murderer was one of Lefty's followers?

Quickly I scanned the names. John Kilgore, Ed Mitchell, Lou Tabor, Dick Stewart. None of them rang a bell.

I jotted them down, making a note to research them on the Internet as soon as possible. If Frank King had found something there, so could I.

Kong raised his head and looked at me with sleepy brown eyes as if to say, "Turn out the light, for pete's sake."

"Just a few more pages," I promised him. I continued to the section, *Tying Your Own Deceiver*. After a few lines of *putting your hook into the vise, catching the ty-*

ing thread into the hook at the eye, winding down to the bend . . . I drifted off to sleep.

The next morning, as I struggled to open my eyes, I became aware of an unfamiliar weight pressing down on my chest. Kong? No way. He weighed less than three pounds soaking wet. I raised my hands above my waist and encountered—"the book." The sacred *Comprehensive History of Fishing Flies* that had put me into a deep, dreamless sleep the night before.

With some exasperation I pushed it aside and slid out from under my toasty electric blanket. I waited for the blast of cold air but was greeted with a temperature that surely reached into the seventies. *Hallelujah!* My heater must've fixed itself during the night. I didn't ask why or how. I probably wouldn't have been able to figure it out anyway. The only important thing was that I now had heat. Lovely, skin-warming, glorious heat.

"Kong, this is going to be a great day!" I sang out, stretching my arms above my head. He stood up on the bed and, catching my mood, began wagging his tail.

Then my cheapie deluxe phone rang.

My arms dropped to my sides as I checked my alarm clock. It was seven-thirty. That could be only one person. My mother.

I debated letting the answering machine pick up but knew I would be postponing the inevitable.

Slowly I reached for the receiver.

"Mallie, this is your mother."

"Hi, Mom. What a surprise." I moved into the kitchen and reached for the coffeepot. It always helped if I occupied myself with mundane tasks during these little mother-daughter conversations. Gave me something to focus on besides my own rising irritation.

"You know me—I like to be unpredictable." She let out a trill of laughter.

I almost dropped the glass pot. The closest my mother came to spontaneity was when she forgot her appointment book and showed up at her hairdresser's an hour early.

"I wanted to let you know that we should be seeing you in a day or two."

This time I did drop the pot, but it landed on a small imitation-silk braided carpet I had laid in front of the sink. The pod didn't break, but the plastic handle loosened.

"Did you hear me?"

"Sure did." I set the pot on the counter, not trusting myself to continue if my mother insisted on dropping these early-morning bombs. "Where are you?"

"Nearby. Actually, close enough to feel the cold snap."

"Oh, yeah, it's been downright miserable." I seized on the opportunity to bad-mouth the island. "You might want to rethink your itinerary. I heard that the temperature might dip even lower."

"It's okay. We brought our winter coats with us." She

sniffed in a determined manner. "We're looking forward to seeing you."

"Me too," I managed to eke out.

Strains of rock music drifted out of the Wanderlodge and distracted me for a moment. Not the hard-driving, punk stuff but the more soft-rock songs of . . . Christina Aguilera. *That's it!* I snapped my fingers. Christina and Jordan Bratman—the guy she married in a fantasy wedding in the Napa Valley. They were my neighbors. *Unbelievably cool.*

"We'll call you. Ta-ta." She hung up, and my attention turned back to the phone.

I stared at the receiver for a few seconds, trying to make sense of the conversation. *Oh, joy.* Could it be? Was Coral Island big enough to share with my parents?

The bigger question, though, was, was I sharing space at the Twin Palms RV Resort with a famous pop singer? Only one woman could answer that question: Wanda Sue.

In no time flat, I had walked Kong, showered, and dressed and was heading through the doors of the Twin Palms reception building. It was built in a large octagonal shape, supported by wood pillars with a split-log roof. A check-in desk stood to one side. The rest of the place was taken up with shelves that stocked various RV necessities, such as biodegradable toilet paper and sewer hoses.

"Mallie, honey, you're up early!" Wanda Sue exclaimed from behind the check-in desk. She was wearing her "church clothes"—a familiar ensemble that included a bright lime green flowered dress, green high heels, and a little hat perched on top of her head. Today she'd added another festive touch—a pair of dangly earrings in the shape of tiny gold Florida 'gators. *Cute*.

"I've got a good reason—I figured out who's in the Wanderlodge." I strolled up to her, leaned down, and whispered, "Christina Aguilera and her hubby."

Wanda Sue burst into laughter. "Oh, honey. You're so cold, your legs are gonna freeze right up to your butt."

My bubble burst, and I slumped into a chair. *Wrong again.* "I give up. Here I am on a murder case again, and I can't even figure out who's living next door to me. I'm some kind of bum investigative reporter."

"Whaddya mean? Detective Billie arrested Jake Fowler, and it's all because of you."

"Jake?" I jerked upright. "What? When? Why?" At least I remembered my journalist's questions.

"It happened like this: I was discussing Frank's attempted murder over coffee with the clerk at the Circle K, when who should stroll up but Old Man Brisbee? He told us Nick arrested Jake late last night on account of finding Jake's fishing net wrapped around Frank's head. All the island guys tag their nets with their names, so they knew it was his."

"Wait a minute." I held a hand up. My motormouth might get stuck in high gear, but Wanda Sue could get a good head of steam going herself, rolling right along like a runaway train. "Let me get this straight. Jake Fowler was arrested for trying to kill Frank King?"

She nodded.

"Anything on the grapevine about Tom's murderer?"

"Nothing 'bout that yet, but if he attacked Frank, don't you think he's probably Tom's killer? I heard tell you had Frank closing in on the murderer's identity— Jake probably knew that and wanted to stop him."

"Possibly." Doubt rose up in my mind like a noxious fume. What about the deceiver? Jake couldn't have made something that intricate. "Have you heard how Frank's doing?"

"They took him to the county hospital on the mainland. He's holding his own. Looks like he'll live." She gave a coy smile. "Sally Jo called me. She drove into town this morning and checked on him."

Okay. "Was he conscious yet?"

"Nope. He's all wired up to those machines."

I grabbed my canvas bag. "I'd better check in at the paper and see if Anita wants me to try to get a quick blurb about all of this into the upcoming edition."

"You're becoming a regular Woodstein and Bernward." Wanda Sue patted my hands. "Things are looking up for Kevin now—thanks to Madame Geri and you. Now we can help the boy start to heal from all this mess."

"I didn't do that much." I cleared my throat awkwardly. Madame Geri had done even less. Still, it wasn't every day that a girl got compared with Wanda Sue's mangled version of the *Washington Post* journalists who broke Watergate.

"Are you kidding? You put yourself on the line for my grandson, and I'll never forget it." She gave my hands an extra squeeze. "I owe ya, honey."

"I don't suppose you'd care to pay me back by telling me who's in that huge RV next door?"

She slapped her thighs and laughed. "You're one stubborn woman, Mallie Monroe. But that's okay. So am I."

"Two peas in a pod . . ." I joined in her laughter, which lasted all the way out to Rusty. I turned my face up toward the sky. It might've been my imagination, but some of the dark clouds were beginning to clear. And the wind had abated. It *was* turning out to be a good day, even though I wasn't sure about Jake's guilt on either crime. The deceiver niggled at me. But at least Kevin would be in the clear—that was the best news.

Humming, I climbed into Rusty and cranked up the engine. It made a clicking sound. I tried again. Same sound. My battery was dead. *Typical.*

So the clouds weren't completely gone.

After waiting an hour for Pop Pop Welch to shuffle the short distance from his cottage to my truck, and another forty minutes for him to jump my battery, Rusty and I finally limped along to the *Observer* office.

When I arrived, I noticed that the parking lot was empty. Yippee. I had beaten Anita to the office. Okay, it was Sunday, but news was Anita's religion. Maybe she hadn't heard about Frank's attempted murder yet, and I'd actually be able to scoop *her* for a change.

I let myself into the office, cranked up the heater, and ambled over to my rickety desk. On top was a sheet of paper with an angular scrawl: *I was here an hour ago. Tried to call you at home, but no answer. Forget the fishing tournament story. I need a short piece on the events at Frank King's bait store and Jake Fowler's arrest by Monday morning. Chop-chop, Anita.*

I crumpled the paper. Did that woman ever sleep? More to the point, did she ever think *I* needed a break?

Cursing, I flipped on my computer and got to work.

In a couple of hours I'd hammered out a fairly decent rough draft. I read it over a couple of times. Not bad. Not bad at all. I e-mailed it to Anita. Of course, she would change the opening, cut down on the adverbs, shorten my sentences, and eliminate at least a hundred words. But, hey, she would've slashed and trashed Hemingway if he'd been working for her.

I tried calling Detective Billie to get a quote about Jake's arrest, but all I got was the part-time deputy who filled in on the rare occasions Nick was out of the office.

I'd have to check with him tomorrow.

Closing up shop, I drove back to Mango Bay and spent the rest of the afternoon reading about deceivers. *Ho-hum.* By evening, I was hungry, cold, and totally bored. It was all I could do to microwave a frozen chicken piccata dinner and crawl into bed. My heater was chugging out only pitiful attempts at warmth that evening, so I cranked up the electric blanket. Snuggling with Kong was the only thing my fried brain could handle. My eyes closed before my head hit the pillow.

The next morning, I promised myself that I would finish researching the fishing fly at work. That deceiver was somehow at the center of Tom's murder and Frank's attempted murder. Maybe I was becoming psychic from hanging around Madame Geri. At any rate, Jake's arrest wasn't the end of the murder investigation—I was sure of it. I was also sure that my heater in the Airstream was on its last leg. I called Pop Pop Welch to come over and take a look at it. He promised he'd get to it first thing after his oatmeal and Geritol.

After a fast shower and hair fluff, I took Kong for a quick walk, picked up the books on fishing flies, and drove off into the cold morning. Stopping at the Circle K for my usual morning fare—black coffee and two donuts—I mentally ticked off what I had to do that day. First item of the morning after I got to work: Call the island cop for a quote about Jake's arrest.

I parked in front of the *Observer* and strolled in, books in hand, drinking my coffee.

"Mallie, I heard about the events at Frank King's bait shop. Unbelievable." Sandy's open face was lit with excitement.

"Then I guess Anita told you Detective Billie arrested Jake." I did a double take. Sandy was standing by the file cabinets wearing a pair of tight-fitting Levis. "Hey, girl, you're wearing jeans!"

She grinned and twirled around. "Can you believe it? I finally fit into a size ten."

I scanned her. "No price tags?"

"Nope. With Jimmy's help, I'll stay this thin." She closed the file drawer and moved toward her desk.

"Congrats." I dropped the stack of books on top of my desk with a loud thump.

She picked up *The Comprehensive History of Fishing Flies* and grimaced. "This looks boring."

"Tell me about it. I could hardly keep my eyes open. But that fly is the key to who murdered Tom and stabbed Frank. . . ."

"You don't think Jake did it?"

"I'm not sure."

"Any other possibilities?"

"Too many." I clicked on the computer I shared with Sandy. "Before I call Nick for a quote, I'm going to check some online sources about building flies." I couldn't finish the story, or accept Jake's guilt yet, until I knew who had made that deceiver.

Before I realized it, I'd spent an hour looking at Web sites. The amount of information was staggering, but I located one of the Lefty Kreh's disciples: Lou Tabor. I found his e-mail address and sent him a message to see if he knew of anyone in this area who might build flies.

Just then, Jimmy breezed in with Madame Geri and Marley. *Oh, boy.*

"We've got a surprise for all of you," Jimmy announced as he went over and kissed Sandy on the cheek.

"You're gonna finish painting this dump of an office?" Anita emerged from her cubicle, a copy of my news story in hand.

Jimmy laughed. "Better than that."

"I finished Anita's astrological chart." Madame Geri held up a legal pad with all kinds of odd markings on it. "I almost missed the most important part: Her rising sign is Gemini—the twins."

"Huh?" Anita grunted.

"We found what you were missing in your life: your sister."

In walked an identical version of Anita. Same stringy hair, same wrinkled face, same dowdy clothes. But there was one exception: She was stout rather than reed-thin. *Oh, my. Double jeopardy.*

Anita gasped. "Bernice."

Bernice frowned. "Anita."

"Nothing like a family reunion to create good karma." Madame Geri surveyed the scene with an expression of self-satisfaction.

I stood frozen in a horrified daze. There couldn't be *two* Sanders women on the planet. That simply wasn't possible. Was it?

"Last I heard, you were in the Panhandle," Anita said.

"I was. . . . Then I went to Miami to run a couple of

fishing charters. But taking out potbellied tourists who are too squeamish to bait their own hooks is a real grind. Not to mention moronic, big-city executives who want to tell you how to run your own boat," Bernice scoffed. "I finally had enough and threw one overboard. And—would you believe it?—that jerk-face actually tried to sue me."

I could see that people skills were not strong points with either Anita or her sister. *Must be genetic.*

"Right about that time, your friend Geri called and told me to come to Coral Island and check out the commercial fishing," she finished.

"She's not my friend." Anita flicked a stern glance in the psychic's direction, then focused her attention back on her plus-sized twin. "I thought you might've showed up to pay me back that two hundred and fifty dollars you owe me."

Bernice's eyes narrowed. "That car deal was fair and square. How could I have known the brakes would go out after you bought it from me? But, since you're working in such a dump, I can see that you need money. Here." She reached into her pants pocket and pulled out a crinkled dollar bill. "Consider this a down payment. I give you another one every week until the debt is paid."

"Dock rat." Anita ignored the money.

"Shriveled up old hag." Bernice threw it to the floor.

"Nice to see you, sis." Anita smiled. "I hope you drop dead before you get your fishing business going."

"No such luck, dearie." Bernice smiled back. "I plan

to stay here a long, long time just to irritate you." She waltzed out the front door with a flourish.

Anita threw up her hands and howled, "I need a cigarette!" Then she stalked back into her office, but not before telling me that the draft of my news story that I'd e-mailed her yesterday was trash.

"It's not finished," I said. But she'd closed the door.

"Nothing like reuniting two sisters," Madame Geri pronounced in a upbeat tone. "It's so touching."

"Touching? I thought they were going to start a fist fight at any moment." I covered my eyes with my palms. "Now I have *two* Anitas on my hands. Thanks a lot, Madame Geri. My situation just got worse."

"You never know. They might grow on each other—and you," Sandy offered in a hopeful voice.

I dropped my hands and gave her a look of disbelief. "Get real."

"I heard about Jake Fowler's arrest," Madame Geri said. "They've got the wrong man. The spirits told me this morning."

Huh? Were we finally *both* on the same psychic wavelength? In spite of myself, excitement kindled inside me. "I never believed that Kevin was capable of killing his own father, and I'm not totally convinced that Jake did it, because of the deceiver. But I'm running out of leads. Frank King was the likeliest suspect; then he got himself almost killed. And that rules out Sally Jo. I can't see her murdering her husband so she can be with

Frank—and then turning around and trying to kill him too. That leaves Jake. . . ."

Madame Geri tapped the side of her head. "I'm not channeling too well right now. I think I'm on the wrong frequency or something."

"Perhaps you need an antenna?"

She shot me a long, low glance. "It doesn't work like that."

I turned back to my computer. This conversation was getting too weird for me.

An e-mail appeared on my screen. It was from Lou Tabor. I clicked to open it. As I scanned the contents, something clicked in my mind.

I sat back and gripped the arms of my chair. "I know who murdered Tom."

Chapter Seventeen

"What?" Sandy and Jimmy exclaimed simultaneously.

"It's all right here." Excitement bubbled up inside me like a fountain. I pressed the Print button. "Lou Tabor was one of Lefty Kreh's disciples. He learned to build flies at the feet of the master—along with three other men. I asked him if any of the other men lived in Florida." I whisked the paper out of the printer.

"Go on," Sandy urged.

"There was only one: Ed Mitchell. He works as a hairdresser in Miami."

Jimmy scratched his head. "So *he* killed Tom?"

"No," Madame Geri answered for me. "He has a child, right?"

I nodded. How had she figured that out? "A daughter. And she's a master fly builder."

"Daughter? But who?" Sandy said. "There's no one on the island named Mitchell that I can think of."

"She married a man named Jennings. They apparently divorced a few years ago, and she left Miami."

"Oh, no." Sandy's eyes widened. "Beverly Jennings."

"Exactly." I jumped to my feet. "Frank told me that Tom had been having an affair. It must've been with Beverly. All this time, we've been thinking it was Frank or Jake. But Tom's lover was the murderer. It fits. She knows fishing and boats like the back of her hand. She was able to motor out to Tom's boat, kill him, and make it back without anyone's being the wiser."

"We've got to call the police," Jimmy said.

"This is all just theory." I reached for my jacket. "We need to get her to confess—for Kevin's sake. She could hurt him."

"Mallie, let Detective Billie handle it—" Sandy began.

"Go ahead and call him. I'll meet him at the elementary school with my findings." I checked to make sure my iPod was in my canvas bag—just in case Beverly said anything incriminating. "Don't worry. It's a public place. There's nothing Beverly can do to me there."

"At least take Mom with you." Jimmy stood between me and door, with no sign of backing down.

I hesitated a few seconds, then relented. "All right. But keep that bird quiet."

Madame Geri squared her shoulders and patted Marley. Jimmy stepped aside. Sandy picked up the phone.

"Let Anita know where we've gone," I tossed off over my shoulder as Madame Geri and I left the office.

We climbed into Rusty, who, for once, roared into life just when I needed him. "Are you up to this?" I asked Madame Geri.

"What do you think?"

I put Rusty into gear, and we headed for the Coral Island Elementary School.

When we arrived, I ducked into the office and obtained passes from Trish on the pretext of doing another news story. She gave them to me without hesitation. Once I had them, Madame Geri and I made our way down the hallway.

"It's almost lunchtime. We'll wait out here for Detective Billie." I checked my Mickey Mouse watch. A quarter till noon. Fifteen minutes. I touched the amulet around my neck for good luck. Okay, I admit it—I needed all the help I could get.

"Did you get a pass for Marley?" she whispered.

"Madame Geri, please try to focus." We halted just outside Beverly's classroom. "We're about to confront a killer. This is serious business."

"I'm aware of that." She looked affronted. "The spirits are with us, though."

"That's nice. I guess it's better than having them against us." I checked my watch again. Five minutes.

Beads of sweat broke out on my forehead. I pushed my curls back with a shaky hand. *Where the heck is Nick Billie?*

The bell rang, and I heard a jumble of children's voices in the classroom. Then the door opened, and kids filed out in pairs, still talking. Madame Geri and I hid behind a potted palm so they wouldn't see us. When they'd left, I peeped into the classroom and heard Beverly say to a remaining student, "I don't have time to look over your reading journal right now. I've got a family emergency, and you may not see me for quite a while."

The little girl shrugged and followed her classmates out.

I returned to the potted palm and my two companions. "I don't think we can wait for Detective Billie. She must know something's up—she's ready to run. We'll get her talking, and by that time he should be here." I motioned for Madame Geri to follow me into the classroom. I clicked on the tape recorder.

Beverly had her back to us and was erasing the large green chalkboard behind her desk. I looked around. The ambiance suggested what educators today call "a positive learning environment." Every inch of the room was filled with bright posters and pictures. Cheery and inviting. Small tables were positioned in "modules" with books and painting equipment scattered across the tops. And, of course, a row of computers lined one wall. I pointed to a large, neon yellow filing cabinet. Madame Geri took her position behind it.

"Hi, Beverly," I said in a quiet voice.

She whirled around. "Oh, it's you. Are you working on another story?" A brief shadow of hardness dimmed the habitually sweet expression she wore. It lasted only seconds, but I saw it. It made me shiver.

"You could say that." I strolled toward her. "I'm finishing up an investigative piece on Tom Crawford's murder."

"Isn't that old news? I heard that Jake Fowler was arrested yesterday." She tucked her blond hair behind her ear.

"True—for attacking Frank King. But I don't think he hurt Frank or murdered Tom."

"Really?" She set the eraser down. "I thought you were a reporter, not a police officer."

"Sometimes I get very involved in my stories, especially when they concern cold-blooded murderers."

"I'm afraid I can't help you there." An overly bright smile appeared.

"I think you can." I spoke slowly, stalling for time. "You were having an affair with Tom. But then he decided to get back with Sally Jo, and you were enraged. You were so angry that you took a boat out to where he was fishing with Kevin, and you—"

"Killed him? You've got quite a vivid imagination, Ms. Monroe."

A blinding resolve rose up inside me. I was going to *make* her confess before she hurt anyone else. "No, I've got facts on my side. Fact: A fishing fly was found on

Tom's boat—the kind of fly that only a master builder could make. That's why you tried to kill Frank—to get that fly. You somehow got hold of Jake's fishing net and used it on Frank. A nice touch. Jake was a suspect in Tom's murder. If his fishing net were found at the crime scene, it would implicate him even further. But Jake couldn't have made that fly. Fact: Your father is Ed Mitchell, master fly builder. He also owns a hair salon in Miami where you told me you get your hair done. He taught you everything he knows about building flies. And you learned well."

A brittle laugh escaped her. "So what if my father is Ed Mitchell? That doesn't prove anything."

Ouch. She had me there. But I wasn't Mallie Monroe, motormouth extraordinaire, for nothing. "You forget, I saw that fly. I know it was your father's design. Only two people could've made that fly: you or Ed Mitchell." I lied through my teeth. I had no idea whether anyone else could make that fly. "All Detective Billie has to do is get a drawing of the fly, call your father, and get him to confirm that it was one of his designs. I'm sure he'll do that. And I'm sure he'll be dismayed to know that his daughter—"

"Shut up," she snarled.

"The game's over, Beverly. You might as well own up to what you did."

Her eyes took on a hard, defiant look, and her voice turned as bitter as a key lime. "So what if I killed Tom? He deserved it. That lying, cheating jerk. I thought I was done with men like him after I divorced my first husband. But Tom didn't seem like that when I first met him. He was kind and sensitive. When he left Sally Jo, I saw my opportunity and moved in on him. Everything was fine at first. He was going to get a divorce, and we were going to get married. Then he started having cold feet. He wasn't sure how the divorce would affect Kevin, he didn't know if he could hurt Sally Jo, and so on and so on." She moved around to the front of her desk. "I took a boat out there that night just to reason with him, beg him to leave Sally Jo. But he said he'd already made up his mind to go back to his wife."

"Then you hit him with the oar?"

"I didn't mean to. I don't even remember doing it. All of a sudden it was in my hand, and I slammed it against his head."

Her head dropped to her chest. Silent moments passed, but I said nothing.

Then she turned her face up, her mood veering sharply to anger. "But then you had to come along and stick your nose into everything. I tried to scare you off with the e-mail and—"

"Road rage?" *Aha!* I finally finished one of *her* sentences for a change. "You tried to force me off the road."

"Bingo. Go to the head of the class." She snatched up a paint knife from the kids' arts and crafts area and moved toward me.

Uh-oh. "I was just doing my job."

"You can blame yourself for Frank. You involved

him by giving him that fishing fly. Luckily, my dad called me on my cell phone during the fishing tournament. His friend, Lou, said someone named Frank from Coral Island had been investigating Dad's deceivers. It didn't take a rocket scientist to figure out who that was." She drew closer. "Too bad he survived."

"Beverly, the police are already outside the building. Sandy called Detective Billie—he knows what you've done." *And let's hope he's going to rush in here at any moment,* I added to myself.

"I don't care." Her eyes took on an insane glitter.

The classroom door opened, and Kevin rushed in. "I forgot to get my lunch—"

"Kevin, get out of here!" I yelled.

"No," Beverly commanded, her attention fastening on the boy. "You're the one who caused all of this. Your father would've married me if it hadn't been for you."

"What?" Kevin looked at her, then me. Puzzlement clouded his small face.

"Go to the office, Kevin. Get the principal," I said in an urgent voice.

"No." Beverly lunged at him, but I swung my mammoth canvas bag in a wide arc and caught her in the face. She dropped the knife. I heard a crunching sound and realized the mammoth load of junk in my bag must've hit Beverly in the jaw. I hoped it was broken. Served her right. She staggered backward.

I seized Kevin's arm and pulled him toward me. But Beverly recovered and grabbed at him. An adrenaline rush flooded my body. I couldn't let her hurt Kevin. Releasing his arm, I assumed my Tae Kwon Do fighting stance and aimed a roundhouse kick at her ribs. It connected! She screamed and cradled her left side. Kevin scrambled away and ran out the door.

"You witch!" Beverly lurched at me, yanking at my hair. I jabbed an elbow into her stomach, and she grunted but managed to keep a grip on my curls. Her fingers remained locked in their intention to pull out my hair by the roots.

I yelped. It hurt like hell. Forget the Tae Kwon Do moves. I stomped on her foot as hard as I could. She shouted in pain and released me.

"Marley, attack!" Madame Geri emerged from her hiding place behind the file cabinet. The parrot flapped its wings, then settled back down again.

Stupid bird!

But the small movement distracted Beverly. I took the opportunity to swing my canvas bag at her once more. This time it landed smack dab against her already injured ribs. She cried out and doubled over. I readied myself for another go at her. . . .

At that moment Nick Billie rushed in, gun drawn. "Everybody, freeze!"

We all complied.

After holstering his gun, he pulled a gasping Beverly to her feet and handcuffed her. He turned toward me, his lips drawn tightly in annoyance. "I got your message from Sandy. Couldn't you have waited for me?"

I massaged my sore scalp. "We were waiting, but then I heard Beverly say she was leaving. I thought she might get away before you—"

"I don't suppose it occurred to you that I was ready to bring her in for questioning. I'd located the sites Frank was researching on his computer, and her name came up. Then Jake's son came in this morning and told me he'd taken one of his father's fishing nets to school for show-and-tell. But somehow it disappeared in Beverly's classroom. That confirmed my suspicions, because I already had a receipt showing that she'd filled up a boat with gasoline the day Tom died." He leveled a withering glance in my direction. "But you couldn't wait for me to do my job, could you? Anything to get your story."

"It wasn't like that," I said. My voice shook, matched by my shaking extremities. Reaction was setting in. "I didn't want to take a chance on her harming Kevin or the other kids."

Kevin raced in. "Miss Mallie, the principal is coming—"

"It's okay, Kevin. Detective Billie has everything under control." I held out my arms, and he threw himself into my embrace. I'd have Wanda Sue and his mom explain everything to him later. "Madame Geri heard everything that Beverly said: full confession."

"If you're expecting me to thank you, you can wait till hell freezes over," Detective Billie spat out.

"It's no use fighting it." Madame Geri spoke up. "The spirit world says you two are destined for each other."

"She's destined to drive me crazy," he muttered.

"He's destined to deserve it," I retorted.

Without another word, he hauled Beverly Jennings out of the classroom, and I continued to hug Kevin.

Madame Geri shook her head in dismay.

Epilogue

"Honey, how can I ever thank you?" Wanda Sue said as we sat on the picnic bench outside my Airstream. The cold spell had finally passed, and we basked outside in the warmth of the afternoon Florida sunshine. We were both wearing shorts—mine loose khakis, hers tight spandex—and T-shirts. Needless to say, Wanda Sue filled out her top a lot better than I.

"There's no need to thank me. What are friends for?" I heard myself say the words, and, for the first time in my life I knew what it meant to care about someone enough that I would risk my own well-being to help her. I wasn't the family flake that no one could count on. Even Nick Billie had complimented me on my quick thinking at the elementary school—once he'd gotten over his irritation.

231

Nevertheless, our "karmic destiny" was still very much in question. *Oh, well.* "How's Frank?"

"He's doing better than a June bug on a summer's day."

I interpreted that to mean that he was on the mend. "Are he and Sally Jo going to get together?"

"Lordy, who knows?" She shrugged. "Maybe down the road. Right now she's putting her energies into helping Kevin get through all this stuff. The school counselor is lending a hand. It turns out Kevin wasn't starting all those fights with his classmates. Miz Jennings was goading him into being angry with the other kids."

"She's a nutcase, that's for sure."

"Thank goodness that crazy woman has been brought to justice—with your help."

"She almost yanked out my one claim to beauty." I rubbed my sore scalp ruefully. "I hate to admit this, but I'm going to miss having Madame Geri as my sidekick. Of course, she's a total sham, but she did help me bring down Beverly. Or, rather, Marley did."

Wanda Sue clucked her tongue. "She's not a fake. She's the real thing. You have to have faith, honey."

"I prefer to put my trust in things I can see and prove for myself."

"Humbug."

At that point I heard the door to the RV next door open, and two voices filtered over to my site. My eyelids shot open. I looked at Wanda Sue. "It's *them.*" The famous mystery couple!

The voices drew closer, and I turned toward the

sound. Excitement darted through me like an arrow zinging toward its target. It had to be Christina Aguilera and her man. I just knew it.

As they rounded the front of their motor home, I got my first glimpse of the mystery guests.

I jumped to my feet, and my mouth dropped open. "Mom. Dad. What are you doing here?"

"We wanted to surprise you," my mother tittered. "A friend from Tampa loaned us their spanking-new RV, and we've been scoping out your little island in our rental car for the past week—just to see if we wanted to buy a place here. We didn't want you influencing our decision, trying to get us to choose Mango Bay."

As if that *was a possibility.*

"Anyway, your father and I are pulling out this afternoon and heading for Sun City. I'm sorry to say it, Mallie, but this is the dullest place we've ever been. Nothing happens on this island, does it?"

I started to protest, then thought better of it.

Sometimes silence was the best answer.